MANFRED'S PAIN

Robert McLiam Wilson was born in 1964. He read English at Cambridge but left university early to write his first novel, *Ripley Bogle*, which was published in 1989. It won the Rooney Prize (1989), the Betty Trask Prize (1990), the Hughes Award (1990) and the Irish Book Award (1990).

He is the author of *The Dispossessed* with Donovan Wylie, a non-fiction work about poverty, which is also available in Picador.

He is currently working on a new novel entitled *OTG*.

ALSO BY ROBERT McLIAM WILSON

Ripley Bogle

WITH DONOVAN WYLIE

The Dispossessed

ROBERT McLIAM WILSON

MANFRED'S PAIN

PICADOR

First published 1992 by
Pan Books Limited
a division of Pan Macmillan Publishers Limited
Cavaye Place London SW10 9PG
and Basingstoke

Associated companies throughout the world

Paperback edition published 1993

ISBN 0 330 32418 7

The author is grateful for the assistance of Michael Longley.

1 3 5 7 9 8 6 4 2

A CIP catalogue record for this book is available from
the British Library

Printed and bound in Great Britain by
Cox & Wyman Ltd, Reading, Berkshire

For Jo and Richard

CONTENTS

PART ONE

WAIT AND SEE

ONE

MANFRED had wanted to die for a long time. So, when he discovered this new pain, he decided to keep it to himself. He grew secretive, possessive – for all the world like an old Hebrew father with a newborn son. This was fitting since his pain was truly infant and seemed masculine to him. It wasn't one of his usual girlish twinges or banshee agonies. It 'was a constant, goring presence; an energetic spiral of discomfort. It was a corrosive, manly thing.

Not that Manfred had formed any elaborate suicide blueprints. Suicide seemed the fool's way to die. He could wait and trust. His pain brought him hope. Invited death was a much more dignified business if it was not self-inflicted.

Of course, Manfred had had many pains and kinds of pain before. He had not *hoped* then. He had tripped doctor-wards in good order, punctual and deferential. He had humbly submitted to decades' worth of doctorly estimates and mystifications. He had been the perfect patient.

But now Manfred had plans. He had no use for doctors. This pain would remain his alone. He could not allow it to be supervised by some beardless general practitioner or some skill-less specialist. He would not let his pain be named, denatured and robbed of its mystery. Most of all, he could not let it be cured.

The old man knew that this laborious companion was the herald of something worse – the manifesto of some new and major ill. This suited him well. If he consulted a doctor, he would be skewered on some model of cureless care, of second-hand decay and death. If he festered in privacy, at least his pain would break new ground. It would surprise and appal. Manfred was happy with this notion. Another self-entertainment to add to his ancient list.

ONCE, Manfred had loved his life ardently. He had loved it like a young husband. There had been many radiant sections. Some of his memories (and as Manfred withered away, he found his memories increasingly fleshed and substantial) were opalescent, euphoric things. Emma had filled his life with whole new categories of regret and loss but she had once made him strong as well as weak. Each slow volume of his diaries was pugnacious and scrutably content. Much, much had been good.

But much had been bad. Much had been impotent and bewildering, harm done and harm suffered. The war had burnt him. It had consumed a necessary, pristine part of him. Leaving his wife had made him ashes. Without her, his life had become a spectacle of waste. For more than twenty years they had met once a month on a cold park bench. Their son, Martin, had grown into a man he could not love. Manfred felt like spent fuel. He did not much want death but he greatly wanted rid of life. It didn't seem much to want to die.

Anyway, it was academic. Emma had killed him more than twenty years ago. Living those years without her, he was the walking, breathing dead. Late at night, he would look at her old letters. He could see now that Emma had always known what would happen. She had known what was within her, what future, disfiguring fear. He remembered his own letters as having been extravagant, impassioned. Hers were measured and cautious, always disengaged. She had been careful to lay few trails.

The remainder of grief is less than expected. Regret is a residue. The leftovers from the meal of another emotion.

Loss had reduced his life to its short component parts. He ate, slept, breathed and grieved. All time was rank with the rot of the past. The world was weary. The trees drooped and the tides were sluggish and reluctant. Even the sunshine was dusty stuff.

Death seemed easy. The old man felt himself closing life in common with the century and prey to its ephemeral decay. Neither of them had made much of it. All they shared now was the late-evening drama of two old fools swapping their ruinous sentiments. Their joint conclusions were fitting. The years to come were blunt and hostile. Death seemed easy.

Self-made death *had* seemed hard once. Before the war there had been the trouble with his suicide girl. A nice enough girl. Manfred's mother had thought her decent and thankfully Gentile, of the plainer type, it was true. In her bluest dress (that brought out the colour of her eyes) she had smiled at him for little more than a year. He was nineteen and she was pleasantly fond of taking off her dress. Manfred loved her well, with tact and solicitude. But the blue dress faded and the smile palled. Until one night she called him round. When he arrived, she just jumped out of the window – backwards, strangely enough. (Manfred used to wonder if that had helped: if sightlessness had made that leap easier.) It cut Manfred, self-blame being much blame. But he felt no fault. Women's despair was an unfathomable thing, little to do with men.

It had left him cold and dismal. His mother had wept so much for the dead girl that he felt he had nothing wet to add. A score of pleasant people spoke ill of his particular dead and his grief became a little grief. Surprise was most of what he felt, surprise and embarrassment. And as he awaited his own death, grief, large or small, was mostly absent. Manfred had wanted to die for a very long time.

★

SINCE he had discovered it, Manfred's pain had grown apace. Its presence had become more persistent, more eternally acknowledged. It had even settled to a permanent location low on his belly, just east of the pelvic arch. The pain hadn't burrowed very deep yet, Manfred sensed. It had not yet reached the true marrow of his gut but it was mobile and confident. It was a sure thing.

It was a good place to have a pain. He had never had one there before, punctuating that part of his fraudulent old body. He liked the way it marked that particular blank page. The ache seemed close to cosy there, skating so lightly on his bowels. At the height of its daily prodding, the pain would become companionable, teasing. It was almost pleasant to sit by the window in the brown evenings and suffer its jocularity, to smoke it into submission as the sky dulled and closed its curtains.

Sometimes, his belly grew taut and hard, like a full bladder or a brimming gourd. Then the pain seemed to corkscrew through his flesh and Manfred would have to concentrate. He would lie on his disordered bed and massage his stomach. He conducted fragile negotiations with it: promises of whisky or gin. He raged and wept with pain.

Occasionally, when the pain came hardest, he would hobble into the kitchen and open the cupboard where he kept his legion medicines. He brandished bottlefuls of aspirin at his abdomen. He menaced his gut with paracetamol, codeine and distalgesics of all kinds. If terribly goaded, he would push handfuls of pills into his mouth and prepare to swallow and quench his pain. He never did. He would spit the tablets and pills into the sink where they would melt, fizz and congeal into a toxic stain on the unwashed plates. The pain would increase, fired by his cowardice and exertion. Manfred didn't mind. He loved his pain. He cherished it.

At other times, the pain was almost gentle and his belly

would grow limpid. The ache would lie softly askew his gut like a wise, slumbering foetus. He felt like a woman with child. His sweet joy at its constant, silent presence. His tender monitoring of its growth. The fond harbour he provided in his womb of pain. All this was motherhood. He nurtured it with the little love he held in stock. With widely opened eyes, like a cat in dark corners, he would sit silent in the gloom, happily enduring.

There *were* periods when Manfred would feel no pain at all. These were the worst times. He would grow fretful and would try not to await its return. He would read listlessly but he would be weak with anguish. Eventually, suddenly or slowly, the ache would return. Then the old man's happiness would be greatest. Each new welcome back did nothing to lessen his euphoria. Prodigality went unpunished. His heart would be high with gladness and bright with hope.

MANFRED was almost happy. He spent his days in solitude, traversing the dingy streets of his neighbourhood. He moved from home to shop to café to home again. His neighbours ignored this new eccentricity. They had seen many such mad, lonely folk. The public glance slid over his shabby, trundling form as he traipsed around, his hand always pressed to his belly, searching, coaxing, calming. He would smile and mutter happily to himself. It was strange. Of all the things he looked like, he looked least of all like a man in pain.

TWO

(1932–6)

WHEN twelve, Manfred questioned his father about the grand issues that troubled him already. His father was fast and sure. 'Identify what you desire. Know its essence. Feel its weight. Make it yours.' The boy tried this. He failed.

When thirteen, troubled still, he questioned his mother. His mother was fast and sure. 'Know what you want, child. See it clear. Then . . . wait and see. Desire is dangerous – it gives you pain. It's better to wait and see.' Manfred waited.

MANFRED'S father was a man so terrified of the dark that he chased daylight. In summer he rose at four and retired before nightfall, straining to remain free of the dark. Winter, with its stretches of unavoidable night, caused him a disquiet he could never conceal. The rest of the household were obliged to abide by his phobic timetable: they ordered their lives to the rhythm of his paranoia. This left the three sons, paradoxically, with a fearless attitude to darkness and night rare among boys of their age. They grew to love the dark. They felt lust for its fatherscaring secrets. Their father sensed their courage and feared their contempt. His manner hardened and his displays of voluble manhood increased. He strutted and puffed. The boys grew. The father shrank and weakened. He grew louder and feared the dark more.

Manfred's mother had been a skittish, giddy girl. Her high spirits had worried her parents as she grew to girlhood. By the time she was sixteen she was almost a celebrity on certain stretches of the Mile End Road. She had famously denied the crustiest rabbi in London by being caught smoking unapologetically on the Sabbath. Her own family had viewed her marriage to Manfred's father as a timely brake on her wildness. So it had proved. Apart from her complete refusal to wear a marriage wig and sundry other small rebellions, her mutinous spirit seemed to have ebbed away. She took refuge in vanity of a character so stern and implacable that it was itself near rabbinical.

She spent what money she could on her appearance and devoted enormous amounts of time and invention to her wardrobe. She didn't seem to like Jews. She was filled with scorn for Jewish men and openly mocked Hasidic youths with their hats, their locks and their struggling beards. Her apostasy, such a trial for her husband, was a source of pride and distinction for her. She considered herself entirely English and Jewish only when she grew sentimental or had endured some particularly galling goy taunt. She aped American fashions and seemed to admire only Gentile women. They seemed more complete to her, more entirely women. They suffered no shameful marriage wigs, no Jewish apology for gender. They were proud to be women and, crucially for Manfred's mother, they were lavishly rewarded for their womanhood.

She wore veils which trapped pale light. Like loyal citizens, wife and sons submitted to the father's rule but it was the mother who was peerless. Her hoarse voice animated, reflected and only seemed to serve. The boy watched her accidental heart. He watched her move, talk and rest among her family. Suffering paperweight shame, he watched their marriage. He witnessed tiny mutiny, he witnessed complicity.

Once, they were walking in a city park, mother, father and sons, uncomfortably sampling some sunshine. On the grass, a young couple lay half naked. The woman wore a blue bathing costume which angered Manfred's father at a hundred yards' distance. The man wore only shorts and lay on his belly as the young woman rubbed oil into his back, his fine blond back. Manfred saw that his mother gazed sadly at the shapely couple. His father muttered peevishly, angry and afraid. As they passed, he turned his face from his wife. Manfred started as the leisurely young man laughed suddenly. It was a healthy, vigorous sound which frightened and attracted the boy in equal measure. His father's face had convulsed bitterly when the young man laughed. Manfred's mother dropped her head and gently took her husband's hand, resigned, consoling.

She was not beautiful and Manfred knew that this wounded her. She wanted the arbitrary gift of comeliness. When he walked with her, the boy sensed that men's indifference to her was a trial. It was obvious that she blamed his father for this in some way. The three sons were careful to make it plain that they believed in the superstition of their mother's beauty. She called them her little men and expected them to make the tributes to her that adult manhood so inexplicably failed to deliver.

There *were* times when it was no task to think her beautiful. When the father was out, she would leave it late to light the lamps and she and her sons would sit in the gloom while they could. She would sit by the window in the dying light, her fingers manipulating needles, pins and small garments, her face collapsing in the dark. As her features grew indistinct, the boy could find her beautiful. He felt a curious elation at these times, watching the vague figures of his mother and brothers, their presence only evident in their shuffling movements and boyish heaviness of breath. None ever spoke and each dreamed their varying dreams in silent unison.

Outside his home, the world seemed like a story. Playing knucklebones with plain little girls, walking past the halleluyahs from the church halls on the Christian Sabbath.

The evangels belting it out. Christians making their noise about their worship. Mr Adler from next door and his rubric of daughters, pale and young. Manfred loved them blindly, wooing them with sugarcakes and laughter.

When he could, he wandered out of Whitechapel. In the grander streets he watched the bourgeois women and their audible courtesy kissing. He watched the Gentile sons and fathers. In those streets, the boy felt poor but marvellous. That there could be such a world at all was blessed and fortunate. It made him feel like a particular piece of God.

Manfred and his brothers had all attended a squalid *cheder* near Fashion Street. Dull years of Talmudizing and old men mumbling pieties they did not understand. The two older boys had gone on to the Jewish Free School. But Manfred's father and mother had argued bitterly one night and afterwards the elder boys were taken from the Jewish school and sent to a Gentile place near Hanbury Street. When old enough, Manfred, too, was sent there. He and his brothers were the only Jews in the school.

His brothers changed at this school. They grew boisterous and manly, avid for the secret Christian delights of such a place. They endured the Yid-baiting with *élan*. Their own brutishness grew so fast that soon the other boys ceased finding fault with their difference. They were nerveless in all the most daring exertions of Gentile boyhood. They fought, lied, cheated and climbed trees better than any. The hatred of their Christian schoolfellows soon dwindled into approval.

Manfred enjoyed some of the fruits of this acceptance. He was left more or less unmolested. Some of the older boys taunted him with threats and songs:

> *The Lord said unto Moses*
> *All Jews shall have big noses*

All excepting Aaron
For he shall have a square 'un.

They called him a little sheeny or 'a right Jew's nose' and sometimes they slapped or kicked him. His brothers did not interfere. Their comfort in the goyim world had been too hard won to be risked in defending Manfred. But generally, the boy was not ill-treated and was sometimes even popular. He was always the butt of many jokes, being young and uncomprehending. But most of the Gentile boys left him alone because he was small and dull.

School was heated words over cowboys or Association football. It was a high-fronted building with a blinkless stare. It was dreams of women's breasts. Celebrity was easy. Billy Buck was famous for his Amazing Fifteen Second Fart: full-volume, Swiss-timed, verified by independent observers. Smelly Watson was famous because his father was in prison for housebreaking (merely fraud, it later transpired to Smelly's lasting shame). J. J. Russell was famous simply for being the tallest boy in the school and having reportedly survived a brawl with a reform boy from Bethnal Green.

School was a thousand deep-headed, thin-brained boys filled with fragile self-regard. Five-sensed, literate and sane, Manfred counted as a comparative prodigy and confident predictions were made. His mother felt that her distaste for Jewish education had been vindicated and she triumphed before her husband.

School was the shadeless glare of days he could not count. It was the shaft of an oak tree against black railings. School was a compact theatre in which he starred. It was dreams of fruitful senescence. It seemed to the boy that the world was baked like a cake and, if hungry enough, he could slice it how he liked.

He had been born in February, that stunted month. One of his brothers told him that this meant he would turn mad and die a violent death. His other brother told him that he had been a Christian foundling with a perfect twin in Durban. His parents were paid two shillings a week to keep him until he was sixteen. But when both his brothers told him what men did with women, Manfred stopped believing his brothers altogether.

As Manfred's father failed to make the money that he felt should be his, the household grew sparser. Old furniture, handed down by previous more prudent generations, disappeared from all parts of the house. They were seldom replaced and even then always with something cheap and vulgar. Soon the house developed a schizophrenic air. The remaining heirlooms fought for supremacy with the newer insurgents. The curious dark light reflected by the massive old mahoganies and oak fled and the remaining light was drab or brash.

The father completely failed to understand his lack of prosperity. It offended some sense of self in him. It was clear to Manfred that when his father looked at himself in the mirror he saw someone quite different from the man that he was. The looking glass told him impossible stories, stories of a prosperous, considerable man. As the reality of his life diverged ever further from the man he saw in the mirror, Manfred's father weakened and became depressed. Manfred's bar-mitzvah breakfast was a poor one. The other fathers were embarrassed. The other sons were scornful. Manfred's presents were motley, cut-price things: an inkstand, a second-hand Commentary, two sets of prayer books, some coins and a single one pound note.

The old man began making plans to return to Berlin. His brothers still lived there and both were prosperous businessmen. His own mistake had been in believing that England held some opportunity for him. He had lived in London for nearly forty years to no good effect. England was a dead country. It was no country for Jews. He was still a German citizen. Hitler would not last long. They could all go back to Germany. Life would be easier there. Manfred's mother dismissed these plans scornfully. With such a husband and such a father, they would be as poor in Germany as they were in England.

The mother worked hard and bitterly in order that the family might survive. When money was scarce, her face would be grim for weeks and she would barely speak to her husband. She lamented her lack of daughters. Whatever poor job their father worked at, at any one time, she took her housekeeping money from him contemptuously. She managed the house without skill or pleasure. Despite her best efforts, a nervously festive odour sometimes emanated from their kitchen. Fried fish, boiled chicken, salt beef, chopped liver. They ate Passover bread all the year round. No one felt themselves poor but she. Whenever their diet was meagre, Manfred's mother was short-tempered and his father was bowed with shame.

But her husband was insulated from his own failure by the failure of his friends. It had taken several years for Manfred to observe how his father always found some pretext for ending a friendship with any man who began to prosper. When the boy finally realized the stratagem, he was ashamed each time his father cut someone who had betrayed him by succeeding. The subterfuges he employed – some imagined slight or moral deviation – disgusted the boy. He began to despise his father.

None the less, he liked many of his father's friends and saw much of them. His father was an effusive host and companion. His *cronies*, as his wife called them, were often in the house. Manfred's favourites were his father's two closest, the two Tomases – Tomas the rake and Tomas the roisterer. German emigrés like his father, they were thin men who talked constantly, full of weird urgency and extravagance. Manfred's mother frightened these men. They obviously considered her seditious, implacably immodest. When in the house, the men tolerated the boys happily but always watched the door for the entrance of that tall woman and her conglomeration of unwifeliness. Once, particularly goaded by some recent disloyalty, Manfred's father lost his composure and denounced his wife bitterly.

'My lout of a wife,' he muttered. 'My accidental error. May our Father forgive me. She was desperate for a husband. Secret weddings and public shame. An ordeal.'

His colour rose as he grew hotter. The unspared husband, he told them of the wakeful nights. The wartime sleeping arrangements in the small room next to hers, refused, humiliated. Tomas the rake winked at Manfred but Tomas the roisterer adopted a censuring tone. Such talk was not for sons. He blamed the period airily. All our wives were fractious during the war, he said.

The three men and the three boys turned round. The mother stood at the door, her coaldusty hand marking its white. Silently, she stepped across the room towards Manfred's father. His mouth opened in feeble entreaty but he said nothing. She slapped his face hard, leaving a coal mark on his cheek. There was silence when she left the room. Manfred's father trembled and covered his face with his hands.

The two Tomases were more ashamed of this incident than Manfred's father. Their shame burned him. Though the three remained friends, neither Tomas ever returned to the house. Manfred knew that in their eyes his father was less than a man, less than Jewish. His mother knew this too.

HER supremacy over her husband grew as her sons became manly. She was almost coquettish with her boys. The rubblework of the father's manhood crumbled quickly. His few attempts to salvage what remained of his sovereignty were unsuccessful. His wife tolerated no protests. The old man's reproofs became increasingly hopeless. Manfred was not puzzled by his father's impotence. He knew that some old grievance between them, some ancient wound, had left his father powerless to resist. From some of their angrier exchanges, the boy understood that, early in their marriage, his father had indeed tried to subdue his wife. He had obviously beaten her. She never let him forget that mistake and Manfred finally understood a childhood's worth of veiled hints and reproaches exchanged between his parents. Manfred felt shame for both of them.

ONE night his father came home bloody and beaten. His face was gashed and blood seeped from a great rip in his scalp. He was terribly pale and his hands shook uncontrollably, so that he could not hold the cup of brandy that his wife gave him. Mr Adler came round from next door, his face white and scared. The beaten man refused a doctor but when he began to choke blood the next morning, they took him to a hospital.

There were many such beatings at that time. Manfred knew that his father had been beaten because he was a Jew. The boy thought it a foolish thing to be. Why couldn't his father simply stop being a Jew? The boy was frightened for his own sake. Because of his father's foolishness, he, too, was a Jew. He did not want to be beaten. He did not want to be Jew.

Manfred's father began to die that year. He was not ill or injured. He merely began to dwindle. The news of the Jews in Germany beat him like blows. As Hitler became powerful and preached his hatreds louder, Manfred noticed that all the men he knew grew fearful and sad. They huddled with their families, sheltering in that warmth. Manfred's father could not do that. The boy almost grieved for him.

He died before Yom Kippur and lay five days in his curtained room. The dead man's sons sneaked furtively around the house, avoiding each other, oppressed by some unacknowledged guilt. On the day they put their father in the ground, some old sermoner nobody knew spoke loudly about the father living on through the sons. Manfred did not look at either of his brothers as they stood over the boxed-up corpse. He was anxious that he should behave appropriately but he was unsure what he should do. He remembered the day that Mr Adler had buried his wife. The widowed man had screamed and wept. He had fallen to his knees, wailing. The other mourners had been visibly disgusted by this ostentatious grief. Manfred alone felt that this was the only sensible reaction to death – utter surrender to lunatic dismay. He knew he could not muster this for his father.

A few months later, in his fifteenth year, Manfred saw his mother naked for the only time he could remember. It was late in a warm spring. His brothers had gone away to Manchester to look for work. For the first time in his life, Manfred was alone with his mother.

The sky had been endlessly tall that day and had induced narcosis in him. He played out the afternoon lying flat on the grass of the canal bank, his arms pillowing his head. Gazing at the blond hairs on his forearms, he marvelled inertly at his own close-up beauty. His flesh and its down seemed immense, perennial; his selfhood redoubtable and infinite.

As evening came, he wandered home reluctantly. The day had been molten and his skin tingled. The boy was uneasy. The day's voluptuous relief had unsettled him. By the time he gained his own street, the weather had broken: the sky was vehement, warlike scrolls of dark cloud winding out. The streets darkened in ferment and he felt a warm wind

17

at his back. His heated skin began to smart. He quickened his pace.

He let himself into the house. The kitchen was empty and the parlour quiet. Manfred paused in the hall. The solitude was unexpected and suddenly clandestine. His arms ceased chafing and he slowed his breathing. The tender sounds of washing came from upstairs, small splashes and the tiny smack of wet hand on wet skin. His mother was bathing. The boy's heart was goaded, his excitement strong as a nauseant. He heard a cloth being wrung, a decreasing cascade of little drips. He moved towards the stairs.

His ascent was slow. The staircase seemed endless and obdurate. As he climbed he could see that the door to his mother's room was ajar. A faint patch of light from her window was visible on the staircase wall. On that wall he could see a tall shadow warp and flit as his mother moved in her bath. He felt ashamed but predatory. He mounted the last step and crept towards her door in unchaste anguish.

His mother stood naked in her shallow bath, slightly turned from him. She dipped a flannel in the water around her feet and straightened to wash her shoulders lovingly. She raised her elbow and the boy saw the hair under her arm, sparse but black like a clutch of spiders. Water from the flannel streamed over her breasts onto the shield of her belly. Her thighs were long and strong, set slightly apart and studded with cooling waterdrops. She bent again to dip her hand and her breasts tremored in the flux of her movement. She straightened slowly, her hand trailing the flannel along her thighs and belly and then squeezing it dry, pressed between her legs. She swept it again across her breasts onto her shoulder and patted her neck gently and blissfully. Her seamless flesh seemed bright in the gloom.

She glanced in the boy's direction. Her expression did not change. Her eyes glided away from his. She bent again to the shallow bath. Her hand swirled in the water, laboriously saturating the cloth. She stood again. The flannel dripped motivelessly by her hip for a moment. Then she brought it to her breasts and washed her bosom. She stopped abruptly and wrung the cloth dry, dropping it on the floor. Without stepping from the bath, she turned and lifted a towel from the dressing table. She turned towards her son again, the towel held to her ribs like a sash. Her eyes met her son's without reproach.

THREE

THOUGH early, the morning seemed to sag and pine as
Manfred crept quietly around his bathroom. Outside,
the sky was drained white, more winter than spring. Desultory spray pecked. at houses and roofs. Slates shone dimly
and the grass bent itself damply. Usually, such weather
would have unsettled the old man but it was Thursday and
Thursdays were cloudless in the promise that they brought
him. Their colour could not be dissipated.

As he listened to the distant, hopeful grumble of his
kettle, Manfred inspected his face in the bathroom mirror.
The morning's cold was sharp and his skin was daubed with
patches of colourless protest. His eyes flicked from point to
point on the slim glass, meeting their own reflection only
momentarily. It gladdened him that his eyes remained arresting. Troubled and luminous, his eyes had not changed. They
were his eyes yet.

The rest was old. His face had collapsed, imploded. It
had saddened him once but now the yearly transformations
of ageing were almost exciting. It was diverting to make the
acquaintance of so many progressively differing faces. A
task to lighten his days. Sometimes, it even made him look
suffering, wise. He could enjoy this.

But his neck appalled him. It was a sack of sag, droop
and fold. His chin dropped a bulbous sail of flesh and stubble
onto his throat. When he turned his head, his neck swayed
and stretched until he resembled a lugubrious, dissipated
fowl. He wondered that people did not express revulsion at

the sight of such decay but he realized that he was not unusual. This was how people expected old men to look.

Manfred was surprised to find himself old. It seemed an impossible, unlikely development. How had it happened? He had not noticed its advent. Like others, he had counted off the years and they had presented him with the numerical inevitability of his decline but the evidence of his eyes had ambushed him quite suddenly. He suspected some injustice. He wondered if other people of his age considered themselves old. Probably not. The common ground that such folk shared was the venue of their youth, not the accident of their decrepitude.

The old man's musings were doused as his stomach roared into pain. The first sally of the day. He slumped, crouching until his buttocks touched his heels. The position was appropriate as this was like acute constipation. A thick club of pain lay across his belly. He puffed rapidly, his wind shallow and unconvincing. Sweat sprouted on his forehead. He raised his head and looked at the ceiling. He started to count.

At fifty, the ache subsided into gentleness. The perspiration on the old man's face cooled rapidly and he began to tremble from the cold. He washed his face quickly, the cold water numbing the loose, useless flesh. In the distance, the kettle clicked and Manfred's heart lifted slightly. He donned his dressing gown and wrapped his broad green scarf twice around his shapeless neck.

'*Shut your fucking gob!*'

The cry was muffled but loud. It seemed that Mr Webb was having another difficult morning. Manfred heard the first percussive salvoes of the furniture-throwing that always accompanied Webb's various disagreements with his various girls. A woman began to wail drunkenly. Manfred wondered what Webb's nights were like if his mornings were so impressive.

'Look what you've done, you useless bitch!'

Manfred lit a cigarette as his coffee cooled. Again his pain flickered in welcome, renewing the day's transactions. His thoughts turned to getting dressed. It would be an unpopulous day, nothing to do and no one to see. His usual Thursday telephone call would be the main event. He would wear his charcoal suit to match his charcoal face.

A door slammed and the unseen sobbing woman stepped up her screeching, seemingly closer at hand. Manfred heard something slump against his front door followed by a series of sottish, vindictive mumblings. Webb's paramour had obviously been ejected. Many of his affairs ended in this way. As he drank his coffee, Manfred wondered reluctantly whether he should make some kind of assisting gesture. He knew that it would be foolish to become enmeshed in Webb's romantic complications, but if he did nothing, the woman might fall asleep in the hall and that would be tedious indeed.

He finished his coffee and went unwillingly to the door. When he opened it, he almost stumbled over the bundled figure lying prone on his threshold. The woman was covered with a dirty sheet and was entirely immobile. Manfred hoped that Webb had not murdered her. Gingerly, he pushed the shape with his hand, unsure which end he was prodding. There was no response. Panicking, he jostled the recumbent figure with more violence.

'Miss?' he warbled anxiously. 'Hello, Miss . . . young lady? Are you all right?'

The figure jack-knifed into a sitting position, still shrouded by the sheet. 'Fuck off,' it said. 'Fuck right off!'

Manfred straightened, terrified, as the sheet fell from Webb's face. The man was puce with causeless rage.

'What the fuck . . . ?' He paused as he recognized Manfred. 'The little bitch locked me out.' This reflection seemed to reignite his fury. Manfred stood aghast as Webb climbed to his feet, quite naked, and hurled himself against the door of his flat. He hammered his fists and feet upon it, bellowing irately. His din was matched by a similar cacophony coming from within. Webb stopped to listen for a moment.

'She's busting up my flat, the tramp. I'll kill her! I swear to God, I'll break her neck.'

Once more he launched himself at the door, flailing wildly. Manfred noticed the young Negro from the top-floor flat standing at the bend in the staircase. He wore only shorts and his eyes were bleary with disappointed sleep. He looked at Manfred and at the obese nudity of his other neighbour. Webb continued his assault on the door, his genitals leaping horribly as he jumped up and down.

'Cut it out, for Chrissakes!' called the young man. 'I'm trying to sleep.'

Webb ignored him. In his fury, he was unlikely to have heard. The young man descended the staircase. He stood beside Manfred, watching Webb's performance calmly.

'What's going on?' he asked Manfred.

'I think he's had a row with a woman. She's locked him out.'

'It's hard to believe he has a woman when you look at him.'

Manfred had to admit that the two men offered a poignant contrast in their nudity: the young man so tall and straight and Webb a compendium of defects and grossness.

'What are we going to do with him?' asked the younger man in speculative distaste.

At that moment, Webb swung a huge kick at the lower panel of the door. There was an appalling crunch. Webb screamed and dropped forward, his face smacking the carpet neatly. He clasped his injured foot in his hands and tried to blow on it while unheeded gore streamed from his nose.

'My foot! My fucking foot. She's broken my foot. I'm going to strangle the bitch.'

The young man surveyed him with something close to admiration. He smiled at Manfred.

'You have to hand it to him. He's a trier.'

THEY carried Webb onto Manfred's couch. Garth, the young black man, was, it transpired, a nurse. He checked Webb's foot, declared that his nose was unbroken and escaped quickly, leaving Webb to fulminate about being inspected by a black man.

Now that Garth had gone, Manfred surveyed his unwelcome guest with trepidation. The man was still naked save for the grubby sheet now draped from his swollen midriff. Though Webb was more coherent and certainly calmer, Manfred was terrified that he would pass out or vomit over the couch. He looked anxiously at his watch. He could see no way to be quickly rid of the man.

'Mr Webb . . . Mr Webb? How do you feel now?'

Webb peered blearily at him. Manfred pushed a cup of coffee towards him. The first task would be to sober him up a little. Webb groaned in protest, muttering thickly that he didn't want any fucking coffee. Manfred felt despair. This would take all day.

'Please, you must drink some of this – you will feel the better for it, I assure you.'

Privately, Manfred doubted this but some kind of gesture was necessary. He moulded Webb's limp hand around the cup and went to his bedroom to dress. He switched on the radio beside his bed to obliterate the sound of Webb's renewed complaints. An uninvited scrap of music filled the little bedroom. Manfred did not bother changing the station. He dressed quickly, soothed by the banality of the refrain. He heard Webb stumbling into the bathroom followed by the unmistakable sounds of copious vomiting. He was surprised that Webb had managed to make it to the bathroom.

No doubt, he had puked into the sink. Manfred smiled. He was almost fond of the mad clown.

When Manfred returned to the sitting room, he found this new partiality sorely tested. Webb's coffee cup was lying tipped over on the floor, issuing a stern chocolate stain. Webb himself was sitting at the table humming blithely. He had wiped most of the blood from his face and seemed ready for business.

'Hello there, Manny. Make me some fucking coffee, would you?'

Manfred picked up the fallen cup and fled into the kitchen. It was past eight o'clock already. He would have to be firm to shift this oaf. He poured some lukewarm coffee into Webb's cup and hurried back to prevent further catastrophe. Webb was looking at the photographs on the sideboard. Hastily, Manfred shuffled towards him. Webb picked up an old print in a tarnished frame and sat down. He smiled benignly as Manfred placed the second cup of coffee in front of him.

'Who's the little girl in the photograph?' Webb asked. 'She's cute. Is she your daughter?'

Manfred paled.

'It's a picture of my wife when she was a young girl.'

'She dead now?' enquired Webb.

'No.'

Nervously Manfred lit a cigarette, his lips dry. He offered them to Webb.

'No, thanks. Who's the old bloke with her?'

'That was her father. My father-in-law.'

'He dead now?'

'Yes.'

Webb seemed more satisfied with this answer.

'He looks a right prawn. Did you like him?'

'I never met him. He died during the war. My wife loved him very much. He was a famous doctor in Prague.

He found cures for several diseases. He was shot by the Germans.'

'A pity he didn't find a cure for bullets.'

There was a pause. Manfred glanced at him sharply. Webb's face was inquisitive.

'Have you got any photos of her grown up?'

'No.'

Manfred inhaled desperately. His cigarette tasted bitter, like blood or copper. Webb snorted.

'None at all?'

'None.'

'You're kidding me.'

'It is the only photograph I have of my wife.' Manfred's voice was scrupulous, cautious. 'She never allowed anyone to photograph her after this was taken.'

Webb chuckled coarsely. 'Was she a bit of a nutter, then?'

Manfred swallowed slowly, his mouth dry. He dragged the smoke from his cigarette deep into his lungs and felt his chest catch in protest. His eyes watered and he felt himself close to gagging. He exhaled a thin grey stream of smoke and sighed.

Webb went on. 'Where is she now?'

Manfred was silent for a moment.

'We live apart.'

'Well, I guessed that, you pillock. I mean, where is she now?'

'She lives in London.'

'Do you ever see her?'

Manfred smiled sadly. That was a difficult one. 'Not exactly,' he replied evasively.

'Do you miss her?'

Manfred was startled by the man's vehemence. He could not imagine why Webb was so curious. Unless it was to justify another of his unwieldy theories about the biological perfidy of womankind. He did not want to talk about Emma and her companion complexities with this man. She would not bear such scrutiny.

'Yes. I miss her.'

Webb smiled grimly, no doubt recalling a grievance of his own. 'Why'd you split up?' he asked. 'Was she fucking someone else?'

Manfred trembled with rage. He had listened to enough of this. His fists clenched violently. He mastered his temper and tried to change the subject.

'Don't you think you should make peace with your young woman?' he asked as mildly as he could.

'You must be joking. I'm going to brain the little slag.'

'Isn't that a little excessive?'

'You what?'

'Wouldn't it be better to find a more agreeable solution to your differences with the girl?'

Webb stared at his interlocutor in bewilderment. He seemed to suspect some subtle mockery. 'Nah,' he said. 'You have to be hard with these tarts. You can't just let them walk all over you. That's what they'd like to do. Don't give them the satisfaction. Treat 'em rough and they never get out of hand.'

'I doubt that violence would beget much affection,' replied Manfred calmly.

'I don't give two fucks for affection.'

'But you must want more than cowed obedience. That's not enough, surely? What can anyone gain from that?'

It was Webb's turn to be surprised at Manfred's vehemence. The old man began to regret speaking in this manner. It was not a comfortable subject and his guest was obviously amazed by such notions. Manfred was wasting his time anyway. Webb's sordid squabbles had nothing to do with him.

'Forgive me, Mr Webb. It's none of my affair.'

Webb peered uncertainly at him. The coarseness of his expression softened somewhat. He shrugged.

'That's all right,' he said. 'Fire away. I always listen to a man's opinions. They don't cost anything.'

Manfred quailed. He had not sought an extended disquisition on the mechanics of passion with this man. He cursed his own clumsiness and struggled to find the evasive phrase.

'I'm afraid that my opinions about women are the product of very poor experience.'

Webb chortled like a coughing cat and drew the sheet back from his grey shrivelled genitals. He grinned proudly and pointed to his penis, lying on his thigh like a stunted bulb.

'See that? That prick has been up more than four hundred . . . no . . . five hundred women. It's seen all kinds of cunt, that. White women, black women, French, Eyeties, Yanks – I've fucked them all. Still do.'

Manfred tried to smile.

Webb continued. 'And all them hundreds of women worshipped my cock. They all said it was the biggest and best they'd ever seen.' He flicked his stubby organ with a tolerant, jocose hand. 'I'm fifty-five now and I still fuck three women a week. Minimum. All them young long-haired blokes are gobshites. What the fuck do them wankers know about women? I've had more women than any man I know. And I've *never* had to pay for it. Never! What you can't fuck free isn't worth fucking, that's my motto.'

To Manfred's relief, he pulled the sheet back over his vaunted, bombastic balls. He leaned closer and smiled nostalgically.

'I even fucked a ballet dancer once. Lovely girl – two foot nothing but she had great tits and thighs like iron. She nearly fainted when she saw the size of my prick. Thought she wouldn't be able to take it because she was small. But when

I laid it into her, she loved it, begged for it. Boy, she was some fuck.'

His face wan, Manfred stubbed out his cigarette.

Webb jostled his neighbour's arm expansively. 'But the best fuck I ever had was with a Jewess. Nine times in one night, straight up. She knew a trick or two. It was the first foreskin she'd ever had. Jesus, she made the most of it, I can tell you. She chewed it good.' He wound up to his punchline with anticipatory hilarity. 'Take my advice, Manny. Do a Hitler. Fuck as many Jews as you can.'

He laughed uproariously. Manfred's hands trembled as he lit another cigarette. It was important that he should remember that Webb was intoxicated. The man barely knew what he was saying. But he could bear no more of this. Not this.

'You were married, weren't you?' he asked Webb.

Webb's face twitched suspiciously. 'What's that got to do with anything?'

'You *were* married?'

'Yeah. So what?'

'She ran away?'

Webb's face paled and hardened. 'How did you know that?'

'I didn't.'

'Come again?'

'A man's preoccupations betray him. A simple enough business.'

Webb was visibly displeased. His face darkened and he seemed to be considering the possibility of a brawl with his neighbour. However, perhaps recalling his nude, roomless state, he thought better of it. His mouth curled petulantly.

'Yeah. She ran off with some Brummie wanker. Treacherous bitch. Good riddance to the old slag. I hope he beats the fuck out of her on a regular basis. I love women but wives aren't women. They're bitches.'

To Manfred's joy Webb began to sob drunkenly. Manfred felt no pity for him and his comic trials. The man was part of the great mindless underclass of England, the most witless and depressing proletariat in Europe. There was a limit to Manfred's fellow feeling.

The old man rose from the table and went across the hall to Webb's door. He rapped on it gently and heard a scuffling noise from within. He sensed that someone had come to the other side. Again he knocked softly.

A woman's voice answered. 'Fuck off, you fat bastard! I'm not moving from here until I get my frigging money.'

Manfred smiled.

'Hello, miss? I'm from the flat opposite. Mr Webb is in there now. I came to tell you that you can leave now without being molested.'

The young woman did not answer. Suddenly, Manfred was absurdly happy. This conversation pleased him oddly – a gallant exchange with some faceless girl. Like snatches of half-heard tunes, it seemed curious, storylike to him. His days were usually simple – solitary and predictable. Most days he would hardly exchange words with another human being. The morning was a month's worth of excitement already.

'Miss? Did you hear me? You can go now.'

'Look, mister, I don't know who you are but I'm going nowhere until I get my money. I'm not a frigging charity.'

'But it might be better to leave now,' Manfred told the door. 'He will only make trouble if you stay. He's very violent.'

'Are you a friend of his?'

'No.'

The invisible girl sounded mollified. 'Did he send you?'

'No.'

The lock clicked and the door was opened slightly, still

restrained by its chain. A pair of sharp eyes, thick with mascara, appeared in the slit between door and jamb.

'What's your name, love?' the girl asked.

'Manfred.'

'Well, look, Manfred darling. I've been here all night with that fat shit. You've seen what he's like. You can't expect a girl to go away empty-handed from something like that, can you? Tell him that he can have his flat back when he gives me the money he owes me.'

Manfred blushed. He foresaw obstacles to her demands for payment.

'I doubt that Mr Webb has any money about him at the minute. He is quite naked, remember. You may have a better chance of finding what you want in his flat. His pockets, perhaps.'

The girl smiled indulgently. 'Don't you think I've tried that? There's nothing here. Be a sweetheart and go and ask him where he keeps his money. Tell him if I don't get paid I'm going to take his place to pieces before I go.'

Manfred peered at the sliver of her face that he could see. She seemed to be quite an attractive young woman. Though she thought she had right on her side, she seemed much too young for the weary doggedness of the jaded professional. He decided to appeal to something like her better instincts.

'Please go now before he comes out. If I had the money I would give it to you gladly. Please, I am thinking only of your safety. Mr Webb is an ill-tempered man.'

Her eyes narrowed at this. 'I don't give a fuck about his temper. I want my sodding money.'

Manfred was nearing desperation. 'Wait one moment,' he said. He rushed back into his apartment. Webb seemed to have fallen asleep. His head lay heavily on the table, his arms crossed over his great mound of naked belly. Manfred hoped that the posture hurt. He went into his bedroom and looked in his wallet. He removed two notes and went back into the hall. Webb's door had been shut again. He knocked. The door opened and the girl's pretty, smudged face appeared once more. He tried to smile gallantly.

'See. I have brought some money. It's all I have,' he lied. 'Please, you are welcome to it, if you will only go now. Mr Webb has fallen asleep but he will wake soon. Please leave.'

He brandished the money in front of her face. Her eyes brightened slightly. 'How much have you got there?' she asked sharply.

'Twenty pounds.'

She shrieked with indignant laughter. 'Twenty quid! You must be off your chump. Twenty quid for a whole night and a blow-job!'

Suddenly Manfred was depressed. Her face had not wavered at that horrible phrase. The fact of her night's work shamed only him. Her indignation was gravely misplaced. *He* had not had the benefit of her services. Haggling over the price of another man's venery was a little hard to bear.

'It's all the money I have,' he said sadly, his eyes avoiding hers. 'If you take this and go, you will be leaving with something. If you wait you will get nothing except more trouble from Mr Webb. Please take it.'

The girl thought for a moment. 'All right,' she said. 'I'll take it. But you're lucky I like you. I wouldn't do it for anyone else.'

IT had taken Manfred two hours to get rid of Webb and a further hour to calm him when he beheld the damage that the girl had done to his apartment. When Manfred finally escaped, Webb was still fulminating, naked and unwashed. He was an unusually disgusting man.

Manfred had missed breakfast and now he sat in Mary's

café, buying a late lunch. His appetite had fled. As he sat over his uneaten food, he had leisure to reflect on the morning's events. It had been the first time that he had knowingly exchanged words with a prostitute. He smiled. He had left it late. During the war he had seen many whores and their many customers. The girls had always caused him shame. They made him feel guilt about the manhood which he shared with men like Webb.

It was a curious business. *Visiting* a prostitute was even more curious. What pleasure lay there? The tawdry sham of a whore's sweat. Masturbation seemed dignified in comparison.

'Coffee, Manny?'

Manfred started. He smiled at Mary's eager beak. He wished that the Gentile English would cease using that revolting diminution of his proper name. Emma had always claimed that it was a poorly concealed insult but Manfred knew it was only gauche amiability. The friendly goy liked to render you as ridiculous as himself.

He swerved in his seat as Mary's quaking old claw brought the coffee pot over his cup. This was a permanent hazard in Mary's. Most of her regulars had been scalded a score of times. One day, some young workmen from a nearby building site had brought welder's masks into the café with them and had donned them in feigned panic whenever Mary approached. Manfred had laughed but Mary had been upset by the joke. Unlike Manfred, Mary did not consider herself old.

'Say when,' she croaked flirtatiously.

'Thank you,' said Manfred.

Mary eyed the pile of untouched food on his plate. 'How was your meal?'

'Very nice, thank you, Mary.'

Her smile became overtly sensual. 'What I like about

you, Manny, is you've got lovely manners. There's not many come in here with manners like yours.'

Manfred blushed uneasily. He wondered how to combine this award-winning courtesy with a request to be left alone. He didn't have to try. Mary soon sloped off to harass another customer at an adjacent table. Manfred opened his newspaper – a declaration of absorption he always used to deter casual conversation in cafés. Sightlessly, his eyes scanned the headlines.

He longed to telephone Emma immediately. But he could not. He was not permitted to call her until evening. It would be useless to try to call any earlier than that. She would simply hang up. He had tried it hundreds of times and failed each hundred. Emma's prohibitions were simple. It was her demands that were complex.

His wife was rationed to him. One call a week. One meeting a month. A cold rota. It was all he had of Emma now. A pale, murdered kind of love. Twenty years and more of a call a week and a meeting a month. His days were Emmaless, bereft. It hurt like nothing should. The wife he loved but lived without. The wife he loved but lost.

There was a stifled scream of pain as an unfortunate customer was dappled with hot coffee from Mary's pot. Manfred concentrated on his newspaper. There was a headline about the state of Israel doing something appalling to someone. Manfred, portable Jew, looked at the New Israel without surprise or disappointment. It was no dream of his that was being darkened. He had seen it coming a mile off. The way it had to be. The lesson learned by the century's victims. The good grow weak and the wicked prosper. After the war, he had lost many friends because of his distaste for the talisman of new Zion. He was almost amused to see it turn sour. Predictability had its little joys. For Manfred, at any rate.

The man whom Mary had scalded was now apologizing

34

blushingly to her. He was quite a young man, balding and bespectacled. Old Mary was evidently enjoying his discomfiture. Despite her campaign of spurious motherliness, Mary liked none of her customers. The man thrust some coins into her hand and fled, his face plum-coloured from pain and embarrassment. Manfred watched as he scurried across the street, almost being run over by a draper's van.

Silence settled comfortlessly on the little café as the other diners tried to ignore the ignominy of their late colleague. Manfred commenced his own escape procedure. It was a delicate process. Mary didn't like her customers leaving. Even when they had finished their meals and paid her, she still took their exits as personal insults.

To leave Mary's you had to sneak away. When you finished your meal, you could drink the first half of your coffee or tea casually enough but it could only be half. If Mary suspected that your cup was emptying she would swoop to refill. With your half-full cup you waited, reading perhaps (few entered Mary's without a newspaper – their lance against her dragon). When the remainder was cool enough to be swallowed in a gulp you could knock it back and disappear. It was no use leaving your cup half full and just walking out when Mary wasn't looking. An unfinished drink infuriated the old woman. On your next visit to the café, Mary would sneeze, cough, spit or possibly even piss on your food.

Manfred sipped his way down his own cup and tried not to think about his wife. He was growing uneasy about the infrequency of his day's twinges. Normally, Mary's was one of the places where his pain would be most constant: the extra load of food always seemed to jostle his bruised gut into some kind of protest. Today, this had not happened. As always, the non-arrival of his grievous companion made him anxious.

He returned to his newspaper. RACIAL EQUALITY REMOTE,

SAYS MONITOR GROUP. His eyes skimmed over the story. Apparently, ethnic groups (he smiled to think that he himself was a member of one of those) had poor access to employment and basic civic liberties. Not exactly a scoop. Manfred didn't understand the colour *business*, like he didn't understand the Jewish *business* or the Irish *business* or any of those other similar *business*es. None of it seemed a problem to him. He liked difference, he liked colour. He remembered England before the different colours came. He remembered the monotone tedium of that white-skinned primacy.

Garth, the boy from the flat upstairs, didn't seem to have too many employment difficulties. That morning he had told Manfred that he was a charge nurse which he described colourfully as a Sister with balls. He worked in a nearby hospital. Webb had already complained bitterly about having to live in the same building as what he called a 'chocolate boy'. Manfred, however, felt that it was a cosmopolitan claim. He liked Garth. He seemed a good-natured boy. Webb's wrath had been complete when he discovered that Garth's girlfriend was white. The old man wondered how they fared in this city with its ranks of Webbs.

JUDGE KILLED IN NEWRY CAR BOMB. Manfred noticed Mary shuffling into the kitchen and saw his chance. He paused lest her disappearance was a feint. CHANCELLOR HINTS AT TAX CUTS. Mary did not reappear and he drained his cup. His eyes flicked over his newspaper (SENATE COMMITTEE POSTPONE FINDINGS) one last time. Surreptitiously, he beckoned the surly young waitress whose name no one (including Mary) seemed to know. He pushed a fistful of coins in her direction and she stared at him in doltish resentment. He smiled weakly and left.

He breathed more freely when he reached the sanctuary of the pavement. For a moment, he considered the folly of continuing to buy his lunch at Mary's. It was more a battleground than a café. But he found it difficult to face the day's early meals alone and he could think of no other place. Besides, he felt a bizarre affection for Mary. He did not want to be disloyal.

Rattling his keys in his pocket, Manfred sauntered homewards in idle fashion. Despite the absence of his pain, his mood had inexplicably lifted once more. Even his age and infirmity were an opportunity for this new good humour. His apartment was less than a mile away. At his now customary post-geriatric pace he had hopes of getting there by supper-time. He smiled at the thought.

In a wood-framed haberdasher's window, Manfred saw the remembered colours of faint, receding London, brown and gold. Sometimes, it was hard to remember that the past had not, in fact, been black and white as people almost universally believed it to have been. The breadcrust tones of Whitechapel shops, the rich-wooded window frames that came from the best Hebrew trees. He had stared at them for entire afternoons. The glass had reflected a boy then. Now he didn't stare at shop windows. He tried to avoid the gaze of his present, troubled self.

Abruptly, small sun split upon his face like a child's slap. Blinded by dust and glare, he raised his arms to shield his eyes. Immediately, his knees unlocked and he stumbled. A rage of pain exploded in his gut like a mad drumroll. He squealed in shock as his breath spiralled from him. He gasped desperately, fuelling the pain further. Pass, he prayed. Pass now.

He was about to sink to his knees in weary capitulation when a tattered collie careered out of an open gateway, yapping and growling at the old man's ankles. Manfred pulled himself straight, shredding his innards. He aimed a kick, missed and almost fell with the unchecked impetus of his attempt.

'Bastard!' he yelped. Baying with vexation, the animal

dexterously avoided another blow and attacked with renewed ferocity.

A man in a soiled overcoat called the animal to him. The dog was slow to obey, enjoying a few more vicious circuits of Manfred's legs before trotting off in satisfaction. Manfred patted himself down and prepared to receive the man's apology with very poor grace. But the man merely grinned and walked off, congratulating his cur.

The incident had occurred outside a butcher's shop and now the butcher himself had come out to view the event. A man with a gory apron and a cigarette in his smile, he seemed to have killed all he wanted to kill that day and was inclined to conversation.

'Are you all right there?'

Manfred started at a new address on this peopled day. 'Yes, thank you,' he muttered. He pressed his hands against his shirt, searching for the pain that had doubled him up. It appeared to have subsided. The crazy mongrel had done him a favour.

'Disgraceful,' opined the friendly butcher.

Manfred peered up into his shiny, smoke-filled face. 'I beg your pardon?'

'Shouldn't be allowed,' continued the meatman. 'There should be a law against it.'

'Yes.'

The man became confiding, speculative. 'They should do what they do in Alabama.'

Manfred wiped his brow. 'What do they do in Alabama?'

'Let 'em swing in the wind,' smiled the butcher.

'I'm sorry?'

'String 'em up. Hang 'em high. That'd soon clean the streets.'

Satisfied, the butcher bade Manfred farewell and slouched back into his shop. Manfred strode on, terrified.

All of a sudden, his neighbourhood seemed to be populated by cutthroats and lunatics. Webb was the kind of man who fitted easily into this world. It was men like Manfred who had no place there.

A light aircraft stretched its busy noise across the sky, propellers groaning. Manfred loved that buzz. It was not like the preying screech of jets. The world lost a lot when it lost turboprop. The day was getting warmer and the brassy sunshine was intimidating. It was not an old man's light. In addition, his charcoal suit was growing hot and he was beginning to sweat. He was tired. He wanted to be home and cool.

But the solitude of his flat repelled him – little point in hurrying back to such an empty place. There was no one to fill the empty spaces of his apartment. A call a week, a meeting a month. Emma's absence had been absorbed by the rooms and the walls as the solitary years had passed. Loneliness piled up like old newspapers – loneliness and guilt. Guilt in the sink and under the carpets, solitude stacked in the cupboards, in the gaps between the tins of soup and tomatoes.

He spaced out those tins to make the cupboards appear fuller than they were. He filled his fridge in the same fashion and meagrely stocked his own small life. He was scrupulous in having just enough for himself. Surplus led to thoughts of one absent. He waited for no one and expected no one. A part of her would always be his and he had learned to manage with that. But when he scoured his cooker, when he cleaned his fridge or his cupboards, he could never quite wash out the old dust of loneliness and guilt.

THAT night in his kitchen, the old man went about the task of preparing the flaskful of Turkish coffee that habitually helped him through his nights. It made for lazy, dyspeptic nights – the kind he liked. He looked at the clock on the kitchen wall. It was late. The expansive solitude of the night awaited him. He often stayed up all night, sleeplessly reading or simply sipping coffee and painlessly reflecting. Since he had been a boy he had loved darkness. Sometimes, he felt that it was only at night that he truly became his own man.

Most of the time he slept, naturally. His memories were an onerous burden and sometimes they wearied him. Sleep had changed its nature for him. It did not rejuvenate as it once had. It had become an impartial conclusion to his day, a luckless appeal against weariness. But tonight he would sleep. It was not yet midnight and the idea of surviving the bleak, sleepless hours before daybreak was empty of allure.

In addition, late at night he was prone to inspecting Emma's old letters and he wanted to avoid the anguish they produced. It had been a pleasure once but he had read them so often that the pleasure had frayed badly. Sometimes he would even pass whole nights just staring at his one photograph of her. He would take it from its frame and sweep his fingers across it. Its edges were curling and brittle, its inky heart fading into pale obscurity. Soon, the image would dissolve entirely, leaving only cracked paper and finger-marks.

The photograph and the few snatches of her penmanship were most of what Emma had left him. They were nothing: profiles, reports, the cream of hearsay. His nights were empty of her and he was lonely. Time itself had changed for him in his solitude. Lonely time was different time. It was not, as he once imagined, slower. It was actually much quicker than normal time. It sped by like a fistful of river. For the lonely, the precious stuff of time went cheap.

He was sinking into torpor when he heard the building's general doorbell ring. He waited in the hope that Garth or Webb might answer. The bell sounded again. Reluctantly, he went out to the hall. Through the frosted glass of the front door he could make out the figure of a woman standing in the glow from the porch light. He opened the door. Webb's young whore stood before him, smiling confidently.

'Hello again,' she said.

'Hello.'

She rummaged in her handbag and held out her hand towards Manfred. He stared at that limb suspiciously. It held two ten-pound notes.

'You were so sweet this morning, I couldn't bear to keep your money.'

Manfred was confused. 'But . . .'

The girl smiled tolerantly. 'Don't worry about it. I got my money's worth out of that fat bastard. Some friends of mine settled his hash for him good and proper.'

'I see.'

She held out her hand again. 'Well, don't you want your money back, then?'

She thrust the notes into his hand. The old man blushed and stammered nervous thanks.

The girl continued in expansive vein. 'You don't want to hang around with that Webb character. He's a piece of piss. Not your type at all.'

Manfred flushed deeper. He saw Garth approaching from the other side of the street. Desperately, he tried to get rid of the girl before his young neighbour arrived. 'Well, thank you very much. It was kind of you to return this.'

'God, you talk lovely. You really do.' Her own voice was dense with the deep sweetness of all vulgar women. Manfred tried to grin but noticed in alarm that Garth was now crossing the road.

'Thank you again,' he mumbled. 'I must go in now. I'm afraid I tire very easily.' He pressed a special smile onto his features as Garth walked up the house steps.

'Well, listen, darling,' the girl said. 'My name's Mandy. Give me a call if you like. I'll give you my number.'

She handed him a printed card and Manfred quailed as Garth threw him a bantering, roll-eyed smile in passing. The old man blushed a third time.

Mandy observed his discomfiture and her face hardened. 'You shouldn't be ashamed to be seen talking to me,' she said.

'I'm not,' he lied. 'I'm not at all.'

Her smile was neutral, still offended. 'Anyway, thanks for this morning. I've got to go. I've a car waiting for me.'

Manfred looked across the street and saw a large car parked on the other side of the road. A coil of cigarette smoke leaked out from the open window and he could see the shadow of some restless ruffian in the driver's seat. His heart saddened for the girl. Despite all her brashness and her saleable smile, she seemed suddenly small. Too tiny to support such parasites.

'I'm sorry if I offended you,' he said gently.

'Don't worry, it's nothing new. I'd be a busy girl if I got riled by that. It's every day and twice on Sundays.'

Her grin flickered briefly and she turned away, pealing a pleasant farewell. Manfred watched as she climbed into the car in her rickety heels. The vehicle sputtered into throaty motion and moved off. Manfred closed the door.

Garth had waited for him in the hall. He looked at the card in Manfred's hand. He smiled. 'Was that the girl from this morning?' he asked.

'Yes. I gave her some money to get rid of her. She came back to return it.'

'I was waiting for you in case there was any trouble,' Garth said. 'Our friend Webb was brought into Casualty this evening. He was knocked about pretty badly. He wouldn't talk to me but from what the doctor said I think her pimp must have beaten him up.'

'Is he badly hurt?'

'Not really. A few cracked ribs, bruises, some stitches in his face. Looks worse than it is. He's pretty wild, though. He tried to start a fight with one of the porters. And just wouldn't speak to me. I've been living here for a month and he still hasn't said a word to me.'

Manfred smiled uneasily. 'He has very strong opinions.'

Suddenly, Manfred's belly began to twitch and smart. Despite himself, his hand strayed to his gut and he winced.

Garth watched as the old man's face became laden with pain. 'Are you all right?'

Panicked, Manfred tried to smile. 'It's nothing. I often suffer from indigestion.' He bent breathlessly as the ache became purgatorial.

'Seems a bit strong for indigestion,' said Garth dubiously.

Manfred stood up straight. 'There,' he said. 'As you can see – nothing serious. I'm quite all right now. Good night.'

Garth sensed that it would be futile to press the old man. 'Well, if it gets bad, don't forget I'm just upstairs. After all, I'm qualified.' Grinning broadly, he took his leave and tripped up the stairs. Manfred remained in the hall for a few moments. He massaged his belly which now seemed entirely bled of sensation. As he opened the door of his own apartment, he heard Webb's door being pushed ajar. He turned and saw his neighbour's mashed face peep out. Webb beckoned him.

'Was that the little tart at the door?' he whispered.

'Yes,' replied Manfred wearily. Already the day had gone on much too long. He was losing patience.

Webb glanced up and down the hall. 'What did she want?'

'She came to return the money I gave her this morning.'

'Oh, yeah, I'd have seen you right about that, Manny.'

'Well, it doesn't matter now. Good night.' He turned away to end this surfeit of conversation.

Webb hissed at him. He had something more to say. 'What did the jungle bunny have to say? You'd better watch yourself there. You don't want to encourage his sort.' He poked his bandaged head out further. The gauze patch over his left eye lent him a preposterously piratical air. 'Listen, Manny. You just wait. I'm going to sort those fuckers out. I've got friends in low places. As for that fucking tart – I've got special plans for her. Wait and see, mate. Watch this space.'

He grinned feverishly.

TWENTY minutes later, Manfred lay in his bed. The blankets had just warmed and the ache was chafing rather than sharp. He felt worn but comfortable. His thoughts were thick and sluggish. Outside, he knew that the night was skeletal with unsuccessful lights; purples, greens and other chemical stunts. He closed his eyes, grateful for his private dark.

He had telephoned Emma that night. As always, she had been silent, mutely listening to his plaints and grief. He had talked long but told her nothing. As always the call had soured his night and made him miss her more. But now his throbbing head was filled with dizzy stories of love without penitence. As sleep neared, a trickle of saliva escaped from his open mouth and made its way down his cheek, settling into a cooling pool on his pillow, upon which he pressed his stricken temples as he faded into sleep.

FOUR
(1942–7)

AFTER Beda Foumm, the war seemed over for Manfred. His unit and two others were ordered to clear away what was left of the Italian dead. It was ugly work. The corpses were lumps, formless as sacking. The uniforms and faces of the dead were monotone with sand and dirt. Some of the dead had been squashed quite flat and mushy, some were tangles of severed pieces mingled with other men's bits. Some bodies had been burned until black and stiff, others came apart when they were moved. While heads and trunks were charred, mashed or simply ground away, there seemed to be a curious amount of hands, severed and attached. Gruesomely, the hands seemed to outnumber the other human remnants. The hand must have been more tenacious than other prized parts. Manfred particularly loathed picking up the hands. Though he wore gloves, lifting the dead hands felt like a gross parody of handshake. He picked them up by the bloody wrist rather than touch the cold fingers.

It took nearly six hours. Manfred's mouth dried more and more each time he touched a new cadaver. The other soldiers seemed to be growing hardened as they worked but for Manfred the horror and fear increased minute by minute. The kerchief he wore across his mouth and nose was wet with sweat and he coughed and gagged convulsively. By the time they stopped to eat, he was near screaming. He pushed another body into the trench and reeled away as a sticky, roasted mess poured out from between the exposed ribs.

Few of the men ate. They drank sugared tea and smoked

45

foul cigarettes. Their eyes did not meet and no one spoke. A small bond of shame had opened between them and they were silent under its weight. The tea they drank could not moisten their mouths and when the blond lieutenant ordered them back to work, Manfred's tongue was still thick and rasping.

They finished just before dusk. The desert was twilit and miraculous; ridges of sand gleamed with late sunlight and the sky was thick with bruised colour. They cleaned out the vehicles last. That was the worst of all. Black pools of gore were all that remained of the occupants of the wrecked tanks. In other vehicles, the metal had twisted and bent, forming cradles around the black bodies as though protecting them in death as they had not in life. Many of the corpses had to be pulled apart before being extracted. They were so mutilated that they came to bits easily, with nauseating sounds. One half-track had been so engulfed by fire that its two occupants had been scorched into their seats, one almost a shadow on the metalwork. Manfred had pulled and scraped off what he could but he could not erase the black mark the bodies left on their metal seats; he could not scrub away those final stains.

After Beda Foumm, the war seemed over. What more war could there be than that?

THERE was a great deal more war to come and the stain of dead men soon became unremarkable. But Manfred never forgot Beda Foumm. The weight that death lent the human form, the surplus hands and the dry mouth of fear and shame. The dead men had been like dead dogs. Milky eyes and dusty, failed flesh. They had not been human when dead. They had been a superfluity. Something to be rid of – dead meat, a baggabones.

It had marked him in some manner he could not understand. As a boy, he had always found death difficult to believe. The living were so insuperably sentient, it seemed impossible that this vigour should simply stop. When his father had died, the incident had been griefless – almost comic. But at Beda Foumm, he had been scared. It hadn't been the stench or the horror that had frightened him. That wasn't the worst of the dead: the worst of the dead was their abrupt, mute lifelessness, their unalterable, untenable fact.

Benghazi, El Agheila, Sollum, Bir Hakeim, El Alamein. Twelve days' combat – four days' rest. Eighteen months of back and forward. The British seesawed between Egypt and Libya, advance and retreat, dropping bodies on the way. It was rumoured that Auchinleck, the British commander, was so cross-eyed that he thought that this was a straight line.

The war had started, stopped and started. Now Yugoslavia had fallen. The British had evacuated from Greece. The Germans were fighting the Russians and the Japanese seemed to be fighting everybody. The British surrendered at Tobruk and the BBC reported that 700,000 Jews had been slaughtered in Poland. Manfred's fellow soldiers seemed unperturbed by these events. They didn't care who won the war as long as they made it back to England at the end. The only thing that worried them was the German bombing of English cities. The rest of their time was spent negotiating the tedium of the desert and the brief bursts of slaughter in which they were engaged.

El Alamein, Bir Hakeim, Sollum, El Agheila, Benghazi. Twelve days' combat, four days' rest. Manfred was an artillery man. Maintenance, stocking, requisitions and dummy barrages were most of what he did. He had been conscripted in the second year of the war (the first year proper, many thought). Within sixteen weeks he had shipped out to North Africa. His eldest brother, Saul, was already fighting in Burma but his other brother, George, had sneaked away to America with a girl from Clapham. Manfred trod the middle path between hero and coward. When conscripted he had become a soldier with neither pleasure nor reluctance.

His mother, who had mocked him for more than a year while his brother fought for his country, wailed bitterly the day Manfred went away to fight. By the time he reached Africa, Manfred had ceased writing to her. Her gimcrack histrionics revolted him. He knew that she had never easily loved him. Now the war had removed her from his life effectively and Manfred could ignore her without guilt.

Manfred was a listless soldier, solitary and abstemious. He was not popular with the rest of the battalion who distrusted him for his Jewishness and his German name. Unused to the company of young men of his own age, Manfred was ill at ease. The other men were boisterously animal – revelling in the licence of soldiery. They belched, farted, swore and copulated with verve. One of the soldiers, a stunted, youthful-looking corporal, made his mark from the first. Sidney Tapper was a twenty-five-year-old ex-fitter from Barnet with a rapacious commercial instinct. Tapper considered the battalion's money his. He was the only soldier Manfred knew who didn't despise the Arabs. They were high in Tapper's international league of smart boys and he knew he could do business with such a nation.

Tapper ran whores for the battalion and many others besides. Wherever they found themselves, Libya or Egypt, Tapper would rustle up some women – 'clean girls at a very reasonable rate'. When in the rear at Alamein, he managed to commandeer a truck to take a dozen punters on a pussy hunt in Alexandria where he had many contacts, impressive and mysterious to an equal degree. Tapper had conceived an eccentric fondness for Manfred and offered many of his grubby services free. He cajoled Manfred into joining the jaunt to Alexandria. The journey was three hours of rowdy nightmare as they jolted through the black desert. They disembarked in a squalid quarter of the city. The place was

odorous, the girls, plump and insolent. The English boys
went to it. There were few private rooms and many of the
soldiers tupped fully in the general view. Manfred watched
aghast as his comrades pawed and mauled the women. One
soldier knelt over his prone whore, unbuttoned his trousers
and ejaculated over her legs before he could penetrate her.
The women themselves were remarkable for their forbearance. They seemed oddly serene in the face of the soldiers'
rummaging passions.

Manfred and Tapper passed the night on the doorsteps,
drinking gin with whole limes and laughing at the complement of stars. Tapper was impressed by Manfred's chastity.
He seemed to believe it evidence of some Hebrew prohib-
ition. Unlike the others he was fascinated by Manfred's Jewishness, open-eyed and näive. He was grimly obsessed with
the Jew-killing stories that were leaking from Europe.
Tapper had a high opinion of Jewish business sense and that
made them worthy of his infinite regard. He was amazed
that Manfred, a German Jew, could fight this tangled war
without equivocation.

'Listen, friend Tapper,' Manfred said drunkenly. 'To
this hold true – the only rule of war. The good will grow
weak while the wicked prosper. That'll keep you right.'

Tapper had one other friend. Spike was a foolish giant.
His stature and strength were as legendary in the battalion
as his stupidity. He spoke tirelessly of his wife, a narrow-
eyed girl in a smeared photograph. While poor Spike was at
war, this wife had moved in with his mother and brother.
Ribald remarks about the wife and the brother were punished
with swift and appalling violence. Spike broke jaws, noses
and ribs beyond number without erasing the greasy taunts
of his own suspicions. Manfred felt sorry for him. Spike's
permanent expression of mystified injustice touched Manfred
and he behaved kindly towards him. Spike's gratitude was
slavish and embarrassing. The three men became friends

without volition and passed the tedium of war in uneasy coalition.

War was boring and beautiful. It was like schooldays with guns and dead men. The fighting was sporadic and most of their time was filled with indolent lechery or speculations on their peacetime futures. Auchinleck had been superseded by a new general, a meagre weasel of a man who wore a beret. This general soon made himself famous for the spectacular victories he achieved by the ancient and respected method of squandering the lives of his men. Newspapers worshipped him and the puzzled soldiery received letters from their wives mentioning the great regard in which they were supposed to hold this flat-headed man. At night, in the chilly, dull plains of sand, the men cheered themselves with fantasies of the retribution they might visit upon him. They called themselves his *bumboys* – his predilection for the best-looking staff officers was common gossip. The handsomest soldiers dreamed of catching his eye at a parade and being pulled from the front to join his loose-limbed harem.

After Beda Foumm, Manfred's comrades stopped listening to the radio news – the war had become fantastic to them, as remote and uninteresting as any tedious fable. Manfred, on the other hand, began to listen more. Now, the war was a story for him. A story bearing no resemblance to his own experience of soldiership. The Americans had landed in French North Africa: Casablanca, Oran and Algiers were overrun. Manfred oiled artillery parts for a week and a half in a dingy rest camp. US planes were reported to have near freedom of the skies over Africa. Manfred lay two weeks on a verminous camp bed in an Australian field hospital, nursing an imperfectly healed dislocated shoulder sustained in a game of football. Before winter came, Rommel had been chased out of Tobruk and Manfred had claimed his only kill of the entire war when he accidently shot an Arab mule with a captured German machine gun.

By November they were back in Benghazi. The Arabs there did not welcome their return. The Germans had been unpopular and the native Libyans saw little difference between the fighting whites. Tapper took control of a well-organised German brothel that had been set up by some enterprising corporal who had obligingly left behind a full accounts book. For the first time in eighteen months, Spike lost a fight when he was flattened by three equally giant New Zealanders.

Winter came, harsher than before. The desert was stung and harried by frozen, bitter winds. Men slept with their hands in their trousers, cupping their testicles for warmth. Their faces were chapped and blistered when they woke. The offensive (nicknamed the Inoffensive by Eddy Dunn, the battalion's best spotter) slowed and halted. The Libyans ignored these infidels as best they could and watched the desert punish them for their foolishness. Days were thick and slow with resentment and boredom. Sometimes a soldier was murdered for accosting an Arab wife. The radio told them that they were winning the African war but someone else was obviously doing that winning. Their version of war was motionless and futile.

In March, the Germans counterattacked. The battles were vicious but pointless and the push failed. The British artillery shelled for days at a time. The air was filled with smoke, black, grey and blue like a roomful of giant pipe-smokers. Spike was so exhausted that he fell asleep on the firing seat and could not be woken despite the pinches, kicks and punches of his comrades. A German barrage knocked out three of the ten-inch howitzers. One barrel split down the middle like an overripe banana and the butchered remains of the gunners lay like blame on the sand.

After more than a month of sleepless slaughter, the British were in Tunis. Manfred and the others stopped at Sfax. Within the hour, Tapper had organized a local cathouse. But his colleagues slept through his cut-price bartering. Tapper took a jeep and went in search of randy South Africans.

The men slept for nearly two days. The Germans had not completely evacuated Tunis but no one cared about digging foxholes. They slept where they stopped, prepared to die rather than dig any more. Tired to foolishness, Manfred slept and dreamed of the dead at Beda Foumm. When he woke, he walked around the sleeping forms of the other men, all so like weary corpses themselves. He watched them twitch and whimper in the grip of their own grieving dreams. He felt pity for them, these sleeping, dreaming soldiers.

It was late in the day and the desert was changing colour minute by minute. Manfred stole some cigarettes from the comatose Spike and boiled himself some tea. He sat on the roof of a trailer watching the desert fade to blackness while fifty men slept around him. The desert was theirs. The war in Africa was over. Italy would soon be overrun and the war might end before the summer did. The desert had been sown with dead men and they had all come back to where they had been before. As he sat there, Manfred did not feel numb, he did not wonder what it had all been for. He looked at the sleeping men with whom he shared this war. Watching their faces disappearing in the gloom, war seemed a magical thing. Bad magic but magic all the same.

By the time Manfred's unit arrived in Italy, the entire Italian army had surrendered. The fall of Sicily had left them with no hope. The Sicilian fighting had been brief but bloody. Stories circulated. A straggling unit of German commandos had fought to the last man with lunatic zeal in Catania. Both the Americans and British had shot prisoners. The war had stopped pretending that it wasn't ugly. The men despised the Italians now – forgetting that they had died as well as any at Beda Foumm. When it was announced that Italy would now fight on the side of the Allies, there was universal groaning. None the less, the men were glad to leave Africa. Italy promised comforts and pleasures which had been impossible in the desert.

They landed at Reggio di Calabria. The Germans had occupied Rome but the men were still confident of a quick campaign. The Americans had taken Salerno, and Naples had fallen after grim losses. Manfred's battalion stopped outside Loggia. They were quartered in a battered little village from which all the young men were absent, fighting or dead. Tapper was desperate to reach Naples. The Italians had a history of trading excellence that stretched back to the Renaissance and the Roman Empire. Already, the country had become an exemplar of occupation sordor. War had made the men cowed brutes and the women whores and thieves. Tapper imagined that the Americans were running around the country with their trousers undone and it broke his heart to think that other men would reap the financial harvest from that.

Manfred's battalion destroyed the little village. Within a few days, the streets and houses looked shabby and ashamed. After the first week, the streets were dingy with soldiers' refuse and the buildings were marked black with dirt. An old man with two attractive daughters was beaten so badly that he died. The soldiers accosted every woman over twelve and under sixty. Some of those women who would not accommodate these offers were raped or beaten. Manfred was surprised at the ease with which men he knew beat women, sometimes publicly. He saw an amiable corporal from the transport corps beat one of the young village girls. She had objected to the soldier's louche cajolerie and he had lost his temper. He beat her about the head with closed fists. He only stopped when one of his comrades shouted some lazy objection. Manfred grew tired of seeing women with bruised faces and misshapen jaws. Something had happened to these men and violence, organized or intimate, had become a simple thing. Officers were indulgent if such mis-behaviour could be ignored. If not, the punishment they administered was never severe – as if the destruction of an occupied country was an unfortunate but natural result of soldiery. Manfred was ashamed.

They were sent on to Cassino. The Germans retreated as they advanced and there was only light combat. The officers grew careless and the unit grew sloppy. Men were killed through carelessness – snipers, mines, boobytraps. Everyone thought now that the war would soon be over and the deaths mattered less in the rush to finish the business of fighting.

The Germans, however, took up a strong defensive position in the monastery on Monte Cassino. The advance halted and the heavy guns were brought forward. The word came from the upper ranks that they were not to shell the monastery. It was too old and much too famous to destroy. The Italians were allies now and their ancient monuments could not be damaged. The men complained that it would take months to dislodge the enemy without general artillery fire. No one listened.

CASSINO was a bad dream. Two armies formed a deadly bottleneck. The fighting was intermittent but terrible. Another bad winter had come and the lines were choked by snow or mud. Sometimes, casualties were so high and the weather so dreadful that the dead were left long where they lay, some disappearing into the mud-slicks or being crushed under tyres and tracks.

The men were stuck there for long months. They grew depressed and bitter. Their hopes faded and the war seemed likely to continue for ever in this mad vacuum in the Italian midlands. Even Tapper made no money for three months. For Manfred, the time at Cassino became a numb aggregate of horrors: the dreadful things happened with the remorseless monotony of a list being read, a roll being called.

THE battalion cook died when a German shell hit the mess kitchen. A barrel of oil had ignited and smothered the cook in fire. His screams could be heard above the woof of flame. The man's face contorted horribly as it burned. A few others tried to douse the flames and were burned themselves. In the end a big Geordie sergeant took his pistol and shot the man dead. The body fell backwards and burned itself out on the floor. Manfred ate nothing for three days.

EDDY Dunn was killed by friendly fire. They found his body in the churned-up mud of a forward position, ripped apart between rib and hip, his hands stiffly clutching the air. The officer commanding the battery which had fired on him wept like a child.

'It wasn't my fault,' he sobbed repeatedly. 'I didn't see him.'

'*It wasn't my fault. I didn't see him.*'

A SIGNALS unit commandeered a farmhouse for a new head-quarters and found the decomposing remains of an entire family, parents and four children, in the kitchen, a half-eaten meal mouldering on the table. A shell had come through the roof and exploded so that the interior was shredded but no external damage was done. The signalmen cursed the inconvenience and, leaving the dead family unburied, looked for another headquarters.

THE Americans had been pinned down at Anzio and stories circulated about the slaughter there. Cassino's mud dried slowly and by the end of April conditions were close to tolerable. They received orders to shell the monastery. In early May, Manfred's battalion took part in an artillery bombardment made up of two thousand guns. The noise of the barrage was terrible. Manfred had never grown accustomed to the sound of firing and each blast was a thump he felt in his bones, like a sudden fright. Each passing minute of that din seemed like the last minute bearable. Some men went deaf. One gunner died of heart failure.

They launched shells in their countless thousands and were badly hammered in return. Command broke down. The infantry began to advance and the artillerymen continued firing at random, shelling indiscriminately, with automatic zeal. They fired on their own men without caring. The assault had taken on some insane momentum and the men worked without thought while the guns leaped and bucked like happy puppies.

In that final assault on Cassino, Manfred learned what men would do. Someone had managed to convince thousands of men that it was in their best interests to approach a hundred tons of enemy artillery in double time. If you could persuade men to die, you could persuade them to kill without difficulty. From the forward artillery position, Manfred watched through the smoke as men killed men with remorseless vigour.

THEY broke through after a week of constant shelling. When the guns had finally stopped, Manfred's ears whined and he vomited spastically. The Poles were first to the monastery. The Germans, though certainly defeated, fought bitterly. When the battles had finished, dead men carpeted the roads. The little town of Cassino was mutilated. The streets were

pockmarked with craters, large and small, which had filled
with pools of green and brown slime. Some few stumps of
buildings remained but most of them, along with the trees
and grass and people, had been smashed away.

Manfred's battalion moved through the murdered
town, glad that they would not be cleaning up this mess.
On the other side of Cassino, they stopped at a German
minefield in which three ragged Italian children had been
stranded. Manfred, Tapper and Spike watched helplessly as
the panicking children scurried towards them. Two stepped
on mines and were blown apart. A Polish officer who spoke
some poor Italian screamed at the surviving child to stay
where he was. The child stopped, a crumpled, tiny figure in
the very centre of the field.

The Poles brought two captured German sappers to the
minefield. They were questioned about the positions of the
mines. On their instructions, a Polish soldier attempted to
reach the child. He trod on a mine and was killed. Under
renewed instructions from the German prisoners, another
Pole made a second attempt to rescue the child. He, too,
was killed. Enraged, the Polish officer shot both Germans
dead with his revolver. Goaded beyond endurance, Spike
strode furiously through the minefield, picked up the little
boy and returned, treading an unwavering straight line.

EVENTS seemed predictable and ridiculous after the gross
assault on Cassino. The Americans broke out of Anzio after
four months of fighting. Spike was wounded, hit by shrapnel
in his right leg. Manfred and Tapper visited their unfortunate
friend in a shabby villa serving as a military hospital. Tapper
didn't manage to see Spike. He was waylaid by some American orderlies who seemed to have a business proposition for
him. Left to himself, Manfred stumbled into the wrong ward
and saw the Anzio halfmen, the multiple amputees from the

beach-head battle. A white ward with a score of beds occupied by mere trunks of men, limbless, bandaged, strapped and bound. A nurse came and chased him angrily. The ward was restricted, a guilty, shameful place.

ROME was liberated. The Allies pushed north through middle Italy. Twelve days' combat, four days' rest. The human consequence was everywhere. Villages and suburbs obliterated, the occasional corpse lying by the roadside. Filthy children. A hundred horrors, a hundred crimes. That summer, the Prime Minister visited Manfred's regiment at Siena. He was bellicose and jolly. The British and Americans were moving through France and the Japanese were being winkled out of the Far East. Churchill set up a Jewish Brigade which Manfred's CO invited him to join. Manfred refused, to the colonel's obvious irritation. He explained that he did not want to be caught by the Nazis in a Jewish Brigade uniform. The colonel dismissed him contemptuously.

The war had another year to run. Twelve days' combat, four days' rest. It was a weary year which sleep could not cure. Countries fell and capitals were liberated in zestless, costly succession. Manfred and Tapper wintered at the front near Bologna. Spike had joined another unit and Tapper's dealings had lost their old pleasure. The battalion had been more than decimated and many of his best customers had been killed or invalided back to England. War-sick and numb, Manfred and Tapper bored each other for a few more fruitless months.

Increasing numbers of their weary battalion were being withdrawn south to administer and police the occupied countryside in the rear. Anti-Fascists' reprisals were common and brutal. Though few were arrested or molested for these offences, the Allies made a cosmetic effort at keeping the peace between the internecine Italians. This work was much coveted: it was a much less onerous and hazardous business than the front. Manfred and Tapper volunteered. When a Military Liaison officer noticed that Manfred spoke German, he and Tapper were asked to volunteer for post-war military service in Germany. Sensing an unprecedented financial opportunity, Tapper begged Manfred to accept this offer. Manfred acquiesced. The war, dull and repulsive though it was, had taken admirable control of his life. It was easier to allow that to continue. He was too tired to say no. That spring, he learned that his brother had been killed in Burma. His mother wrote him a bitter letter, blaming him obscurely for Saul's death. Manfred could not feel that this was unjust. The war had shown him how everyone could be blamed for everything, how everyone's hands were dirty. Saul's anonymous death was no surprise or injury. He felt nothing but the shame of feeling nothing.

As April came again, there was fighting on the Gothic Line in the North but Manfred and Tapper found that their conditions improved enormously in the rear. Their duties were light. They ate and slept well. Tapper even allowed himself to sleep with one of his girls and was fellated for the first time by a high-altitude Italian blonde who greatly praised the beauty of the single freckle on his penis. To Manfred's amazement, Tapper told him that he had paid the girl. That counted for some kind of needless gallantry with Tapper.

THE war was dying. Mussolini and Clara Petacci were caught, killed and hung like pigs, upside down in Milan. Manfred could bear Italy no longer. War had rotted the country and it was unwilling to feel any shame or grief. Manfred was tired of the dead churches and skulking priests, the villages that had murdered their Fascists when they had deemed it prudent to do so. When the war finally ended and the Americans had dropped their big new bang on Japan, Manfred was glad to leave.

Europe – tattered, dirty and strewn with graves – Europe celebrated. Drunk with butchery, the world had been liberated from thrall. Cityfuls of men and women had been eradicated but the culling hadn't been total. That was enough to celebrate. Flags flew and bells rang. Victory seemed complete. Democracy was triumphant. Justice was replete.

But the dead were legion, Hebrew and Gentile. The dead ranked in reasonless millions. They were the habitués of nightmare, fallen, bereft. There was no shelter from the great reproof of the futile dead. The living cheered and sang so that they might not hear. Celebration was an analgesia, a guilty narcosis. The world had become a bone box, a charnel ground. No banner, no winner's standard could be raised unstained.

MANFRED and Tapper flew to Berlin in a clapped-out Dakota painted silver and black. They had signed up for a further two years of service. As they flew through the pleats of faint cloud over Berlin, they saw that this city, too, had been savaged by war. From the air, Berlin looked like a thousand Cassinos, stricken and wounded. Manfred and Tapper exchanged glances. It seemed the long way round to standing still.

PART TWO

PROFIT AND LOSS

FIVE

ONCE again, the train dipped into darkness. The dull-coloured cables stapled to the tunnel wall wheeled past the carriage windows in a vertiginous, impartial blur. Manfred's face appeared painted on the black window opposite, grey and shimmering to the rattling of the train. The old man's eyes struggled to dim to the nicotine tones of the carriage striplights. In an adjacent seat, a drunken West Indian spat ferociously onto the slats of the carriage floor. Reluctant curiosity drew Manfred's gaze to its slimy site. The man growled some incomprehensible phrase at him, perhaps an invitation to comment. Manfred turned away.

The old man sat calmly in the expressive gloom. The carriage was scattered with other desultory passengers, frowsy and depressing. To pass the cigaretteless journey, he observed his fellow travellers. He noticed a sternly mountainous middle-aged lady who was sitting to his left on the seat opposite. She was a fleshy monument, replete in the pride of her obesity. The carapace of flesh on her neck even had a vaguely Elizabethan air and her pink, pouchy face was brutal and prohibitive.

She noticed Manfred's appalled gaze and frowned beadily, her blob of forehead wrinkling imperfectly. She glanced contemptuously at the old man's feet and looked away with a sneer. Manfred threw a checking glance at his footwear. Ah, brown. Foolish. Charcoal suit, brown shoes – that was an oversight. It also occurred to him that his Homburg was bottle green, hardly blending well. He was conscious of appearing ridiculous and wished that he had taken more care. It was a special day. He liked to look his best.

But he was always nervous on the days when he was to meet Emma. It was difficult to concentrate. The mornings often passed in a haze of fear and anticipation, his heart sick and lurching as a schoolboy Romeo's. It was important to prepare. Today, though the day was cold, he was gloveless. When they met, Emma always took his hands in hers. He did not want his hands to be insulated on this, the best of all their days. They had to be touchready. Cold to be warmed. Cool to be kindled.

Holloway Road. The station zipped past. Small groups of people drifted towards the stream of carriages as they slowed. The black man lurched to his feet and advanced towards the carriage doors at the drunk's permanently oblique angle. Manfred's fat lady snorted in voluble distaste. The entire globe of her face pursed in disapproval. She seemed to feel much worthy of her indignation. Manfred liked this attitude. She was the complete commentator.

The train stopped, the doors opened and the lunatic Negro belched out onto the platform. He wheeled around in some confusion, mumbling thick protests to himself. He seemed ignorant of the identity of the station and tried to ask a boarding teenager. The youngster stepped around him, tolerant and unconcerned. The snubbed wino sent a long foraging call echoing around the grimy platform. Receiving no answer, he staggered directionlessly.

A young couple boarded the train. The boy was handsome in regulation young disorder but the girl was breathtaking, her slender skirt and healthy, wheat-coloured hair. They sat directly opposite Manfred, the boy flanked by the disapproving matron and the girl's knees a foot from Manfred's own. The fat woman settled further into her seat with an angry movement, leaning as far away from the young man as possible. Manfred tried not to look at the girl.

His chest wall felt rawboned with pain. Her beauty scalded him.

The drunken West Indian veered back onto the train just as the carriage doors were closing. The sleeve of his donkey jacket was nipped by the rubber edges of the doors and he yelped in annoyance as he struggled to free himself. His thick cries were stark and embarrassing in the murmuring courtesy of carriage noise. The man pulled his sleeve free and sat down, lapsing into outraged silence. The fat lady bristled further and Manfred's hands assuaged his aching gut.

The train chugged into sluggish movement, its engine groaning into the upper range of each gear before jolting into a happier ratio. The passengers' heads swayed and rocked comically with each recoil. The fat woman oscillated visibly and Manfred himself witnessed each judder through the answering copy of his gut.

In front of him, the girl turned to her slovenly beau. Her breath flicked his hair as she whispered something close to his face. In the paranoia induced by all whispers, Manfred suspected mockery. He felt the breadth of his misery widen further. His father had been haunted by *doppelgängers* and the terror that they provoked. As a child, Manfred had found this comic, another detriment to his father's dignity. But since he had left his wife, anyone he saw who bore a trace of her features disinterred the weight of his loss. They were ghosts, soulstealers. The girl in front of him was a replica of a younger Emma. Her face, her hair, her very postures were facsimiles of his wife thirty years before. It wounded him that he should see this history-faced girl today – when he was so keen to meet the original imprint of those grave, perplexing features.

Of course, in the past few decades Manfred had seen scores of women and girls who reminded him of his touched, broken love. But it had rarely been so poignantly exact. It brought an unexpected and heady rush of memory.

Recollections of places and events that he had forgotten. It cut him sharp to realize briefly how much of Emma he had lost to the unremembered past. Just as this girl would lose her youth to the same. Perhaps to the imperfect recollections of the young man beside her.

Wary of his absorption becoming too apparent, Manfred switched his gaze to the fat lady. The derelict black man had sat on the seat on her left and she barely knew which way to lean. Her aversion to the drunk struggled with her distaste for the boy sitting on her other side. The ragged West Indian attempted to strike up an amicable chat and her eyes paled, flinty with disgust. She crossed her legs grimly, the supernumerary flesh on her vast thighs cascading through her nylon trousers. Manfred smiled to see her England crumble into ruin before her gimlet gaze. Blacks, youths and Jews. She could scarcely have wished for a more precise conglomeration of her unwelcome.

He found himself staring at the girl once more. Her brown eyes were almost matt in their darkness, absorbing light – like all beauty, giving no return. Beautiful women always made the old man think of death. In beauty's present, he mostly saw its future. Age, decay and death. These were the golden mean of beauty's brief shelf-life. Perfection always provoked thoughts of its spoiling. Beauty disfigured, it was treated differently. Manfred himself had summed up this girl by her face and form. That was a part not the whole. The prejudice suffered by the beautiful was not much different from that suffered by the ugly. Comely or plain, women were obscured by the architecture of their flesh. Beauty was no true boon.

'Hrnthmnth garrgthh tthhhee bbbhhhrrraggghnnm,' trilled the drunk. He swivelled in his seat to bestow a fraternal smile upon the fat woman (massively obscured by the architecture of her flesh). Another frown ruffled her huge face as his stubby brown fingers flickered in native hyperbole. She grasped her stiff handbag tightly. 'Nrrggtgth garrfgghhh mnrghh,' he said. He smiled happily. His was a sunny oblivion and he sought to share the jocular truths that had come to him in his looser thoughts. He turned to face the new station that had begun to slip into view behind him. Caledonian Road. Recognition lit upon him like grubby sunshine and his way appeared clearer now. Bidding an emotional but dignified farewell to his rotund neighbour, he gained his feet and tripped doorwards. The young man looked on with amusement. The girl turned away, uninterested in this low-life opera.

The train stopped and lightened its load. The mad wino disembarked with greater certainty this time. At his exit, the fat woman muttered bitterly that such *creatures* shouldn't be allowed to travel with decent people. Manfred, carefully unjudging, smirked feebly. Who was he to compute, rate or quantify the guilty and the innocent?

A tiny pocket of tawdry Londoners boarded and the train set off once more. Caledonian Road ebbed away, a memory of grime and tile. Manfred shifted uncomfortably in his seat. It was becoming difficult to prevent his innocuous eyes from straying to the girl barely three feet in front of him. He noticed that the young man was watching him. The boy slipped his arm around the girl and drew her closer to him in a clearly proprietory gesture. Manfred's eyes lowered and he inspected his guiltless shoes once more.

The old man was becoming oppressed by this pair's glare of youth. He recalled the days when youth had pushed all but particularly jostled him. He, too, had been jealous, frenetically possessive. The merest glance had been an incitement to hatred. It amused him to draw such parallels between himself and the young man. They already shared much in their respective *doppelgänger* loves.

The train decelerated. Momentarily, the carriage went black. When the lights ticked back into life, the train had halted silently in the featureless dark of mid-tunnel. Immediately, half-hearted conversations drained into silence and people grew restless. All eyes searched for the floor, with the exception of the corpulent matron who continued to inspect the faces, clothes and fingernails of her fellow passengers. She was keen to show how imperturbable she was. Silently, Manfred damned her fat eyes.

As the halt lengthened, Manfred began to worry that he might be late for his meeting with his wife. Some of these tunnel stops could last thirty minutes or more. He could not bear to be late. Whenever he was late, Emma did not wait and that always occasioned him more grief and anger than he would have thought possible. He looked at his watch.

The young couple began another whispered conference, their shiny heads together, arrogant with health. The young man's eyes swept over Manfred, hostile and appraising. His face was blotching into a nasty tinge denoting anger. The old man lowered his gaze pacifically. Unavoidably, the girl's shapely legs filled his vision. Manfred sensed her companion bristling further. The silence was dreadful. Fervently, the old man prayed that the train might move on as quickly and noisily as possible.

The young man muttered some loud imprecation. Involuntarily, Manfred glanced up and found the girl's eyes on his. Her expression was neutral, uncomprehending. The old man's throat contracted in panic. The boy sneered. Manfred was conscious of the youth's disgust for him. Ludicrously, the old man's left knee began to tremble madly. He crossed his right leg over his left in an effort to smother the comic motion but now both legs shuddered uncontrollably. Encouraged, the young man released the girl from his embrace and leaned towards Manfred.

'Got an eyeful, have you, you dirty old fuck?'

Manfred gulped, limp with shock. The entire population of the carriage stared at him, perked up a little by the incident. The old man was ashamed and terrified. It was unfair. Blushing deeply, he struggled to find his voice. The boy challenged him again, his eyes glittering with righteous aggression.

'Well, asshole?'

Manfred tried to say that he had done nothing wrong. But the words were lost as the engine barked back into gear and the train began to move. His head jolted backwards and he was aware of having sounded quite insane, the typical pervert. The youth laughed coarsely and sat back, satisfied. His arms slipped protectively around the girl's shoulders once more. Sweat sprouted on the old man's forehead. The large woman stared at Manfred with unconcealed triumph. The incident had obviously borne out most of her suspicions about him. She seemed delighted to have them so completely confirmed.

To Manfred's relief, the train pulled into King's Cross. The young couple left the train, the boy leaving Manfred with one final, valedictory snigger. Manfred felt crushed with shame. The brief draught of station air swept kindly across his face, bringing some relief and the train shunted off again.

Manfred breathed easier now. He could scarcely believe what had happened. He remembered with unwelcome clarity that he had done something similar on several occasions. He had confronted men whom he thought were leching at Emma. He had nearly attacked one decrepit old man in a café in Soho. Perhaps that poor old wreck had only been recalling his own lost version of Emma.

Again, Manfred inspected his face in the glass of the opposite window. The young man's disgust had not been unreasonable. He was, in truth, a pathetic figure. He was just old, comically old. To the young, the old all looked the same – sexless, unsingular. He even had an old man's nose now. His nose had changed horribly. It had erupted into aged drinker's puce. When he had been young, such organs had made him nauseous. And now he had one of his own. He could inspect that sensation from the other angle – from the inside looking out. He was startling, eye-catchingly repulsive, a veritable goblin of a man.

When Manfred was sixteen, Tom Richler, a school friend, had taken him to visit Richler's ancient grandfather who lived in a boarding house in Portsmouth. The old man stoutly claimed to be more than one hundred years old, though the family knew him to be nearer ninety-five. Ignoring Tom's frowns, Manfred had asked the grandfather how it felt to be so old.

'You young men are ghosts to me. Dreams.' The old man had smiled. 'Your world is unreal. Most of the people with whom I once shared the world are dead. You think me alone and defunct. But for me, it is you who do not properly exist.'

Manfred's sense of obsolescence had no such comforts. The boy he had just encountered had been all too real. It was Manfred himself who was ephemeral to them. He was exiled from their actual, participating world. It would seem that he was no longer even allowed to look. Even his height was betraying him. He had once been medium height but now he was undersized. The young grew tall, women and men. Schoolchildren overlooked him now. He hadn't actually shrunk. He didn't need to shrink – the world was just growing without him.

He looked across at the fat woman. She found age and ugliness a meagre cross to bear. The old man smiled sweetly at her. He looked at his hands, he looked at his feet. He looked across to the reflection in the window. He was old. He was flabby and sick and withering but he was still *there*. It was still his world too.

*

THE rain had eased, a faint spray in the dull air. The tarmac paths of Hyde Park sparkled as Manfred's brown shoes stepped their length. The gloom of cloud was higher in the sky and Manfred was happy again. His gait broadened into a stroll. It was the kind of morning when it was good to be old. Vigour had no true place on a morning as lustreless as this.

He looked across at the muffled stripe of Park Lane where men in suits walked slow, talking their business. He wondered whether the rain might keep Emma away. It was unlikely but he tortured himself briefly with the possibility. A tiny scrap of pain curled itself in his stomach. His step faltered and quickened again. The twinge evaporated. He debated whether he should tell Emma about his pain. It was a futile thought, an answered question. He knew that he would not.

A man and his dog traipsed into view. The creature was large, a labrador perhaps. Its broad velvet head was damp with the day's mire and its spirits seemed low. This was an exercise more for master than mutt. Though un-leashed, the dog trotted glumly beside its owner, spurning the freedom of the grass. Manfred smiled at this harmless folly. He understood the animal's reluctance.

'Lovely morning,' offered the man as he passed. Manfred started, unused to friendly address in the centre of the city. 'Yes. Yes . . . it is,' he called back clumsily. The man did not hear him. He and his dog dawdled on, no doubt offended by Manfred's apparent lack of courtesy. The day's small exchanges were proving a problem already.

Manfred stopped at a convergence of paths. The tiny crossroads was familiar to him. He always turned left so that he might approach their bench from the opposite direction to the path that Emma took. The arrangement was discreet, unspoken. He had often been tempted to turn right and take the path that Emma would take. He never did but the choice, the possibility, pleased him. He turned left.

His scalp began to itch under the brim of his Homburg. His fingers slipped underneath the hat and rubbed his temples cool. It was an act that always soothed him disproportionately. A passing woman smiled agreeably at what she had taken to be such an old-fashioned courtesy. Manfred settled his hat to a dignified angle and pocketed his cold hands.

As he walked, it occurred to him that he had never dreamed that he and Emma would end up like this, meeting briefly in this furtive manner. When they were younger, their notions of their own ageing were sentimental tableaux of jocular crones surrounded by several generations of grateful offspring. Nothing could have hinted at the dislocated solitude of the eventual truth. He would not have thought it possible then. Even now, it was hard to comprehend. Likelihood had defeated him with all its stern mathematics. It had robbed his dreams of graciousness, rendering them stop-gap, hopalong things. Likelihood had made him look a fool.

As he rounded a curve in the path, their bench came into view. He saw the seated figure of a woman wearing a dark overcoat. It was Emma. She had arrived before him. His pulse picked up its pace and his mouth dried with sudden pleasure. She had arrived before him. His step became stately. Heart in mouth, he walked up to the bench and sat down.

There was silence. Manfred cleared his throat, fighting the nervous throb in his head. He had been careless of raindrops on the bench when he sat down and the icy moisture had already begun to seep through his trousers, chilling his legs. In the distance, he saw a frozen tramp dipping into a park bin. It was an oddly reassuring sight. Manfred sighed and spoke to his wife.

'I wasn't sure that you would come,' he said.

THE old man remained sitting on the bench until well after Emma had left. The air had slowly shed its moisture, drying to greater cold. Manfred clasped his chapped hands. Despite the chill, his forehead still sweated. He bared his head and rubbed his brow again. At his feet, he spotted a slender worm of paper bearing the legend: TO OPEN, TEAR ALONG THIS PERFORATION/GRASP CONTENTS AND TEAR THEM OUT.

As always, the old man felt bruised by the meeting. The silences had been longer than usual as they had both fumbled sorrowfully for neutral words. They had talked much of Martin and Julia, his wife. Manfred regretted this. His son interested him less each day. The superstition of parental sentiment rarely survived the adulthood of the off-spring. Manfred could not love his son. Emma was conscious of this but ignored it as she ignored so much else. It was part of the complex protocol of their meetings that it should be so.

Whatever they had talked of, Manfred had not looked at her. He had not seen his wife's face for more than twenty years. He was not allowed to look at her. It was part of why she had left him (for, though he had walked out, it was she who had truly *left* him). Once a month, Manfred sat on this bench, his face turned from her, his eyes blind and wet. At first hard to bear, the embargo, the sightlessness had soon become natural. It was almost confessional. Like a Christian, he talked penitently to his unseen wife. She would take his hand, gloved or bare. He would feel dry warmth, solid and marvellous.

If it rained heavily, she would not come. There had

been days when he sat for an hour as it rained or snowed or blustered heavy wind and the park had shuddered at his solitary figure. He did not fully know why she continued to meet him in this way. After the first dozen meetings, the pattern was unalterable. It became a way of measuring his life. It had the flimsy logic of addiction.

As always on these days, his neck ached. His hand cradled the nape soothingly. It was hard for him not to turn his head towards her when she spoke. The muscles in his neck would knot as he fought the instinct to look at her and see the other stories that her face would tell. He knew that if he tried to sneak a glance at her, she would simply get up and walk away. She had done so many times. He knew that she watched him constantly and minutely, ensuring his blindness. He was always conscious of her invisible scrutiny. His face would feel ticklish and uneasy as he imagined her eyes tracing and retracing its outline.

He surprised himself by how seldom he wondered what Emma looked like now. The Emma-like girl he had seen on the tube train changed this. He speculated. When Emma was that girl's age she had been incomparable, maddening to behold. She had harboured a whisper of other beauties. Her face had been a landscape – a pleasure-map recalling trees, cigarettes, fine meals and other happinesses. Manfred's own sallow face was a ruin now but Emma would not have changed to that degree. She would still hold traces of what she had been. Her similarity to the girl on the train would still be strong.

On the other side of the park, rendered mute by distance, a tiny flock of birds took flight. Idly, Manfred wondered how far they had come from their winter grounds. If he had been a bird, he would have stayed there. A tall, thin young man trotted past him, his sinewy bare legs steaming slightly. Everyone seemed mobile but Manfred. He sat back, locking his ankles and crossing his feet.

It meant little now to Manfred that he could not see Emma. He had never really seen her. She had always been too much in his thoughts. She had been obscured by the patterns of obsession that he had woven around her. When she was pregnant, he had once glanced at her lying on the couch by the piano and been struck by the strangeness of having this woman, this childbearing otherness in his home. For that moment, Emma had been someone else. He realized that when he looked at her and loved her, he had mostly seen and loved himself. On the couch that day, he had been struck and hurt by her otherness. Then, with speed, it had made him love her more. That moment of her isolation, of perfect tiny selfhood, burned his heart.

He had not told Emma about the girl on the train. He had been unsure of what her reaction might be. He said little to her now that might go awry. Emma's moods were crosswords, cryptic or quick. Today, she had told him that he looked ill. Manfred had replied that he was recovering from a chill and, momentarily, Emma had pursued this obvious falsehood. Despite himself, the shadow in Manfred's heart had nearly lifted at that. But Emma quickly lost interest and changed the subject.

The old man began to think of going home. The damp wood beneath his legs was still cold and his thighs were now deeply chilled. He knew that this discomfort would cause him thorns of pain later but for now he was insensible to any inflammatory excess. He was happy to sit longer. It was pleasant to be so briefly free of pain and his shoulder still reverberated from the touch of her body beside him. Her warmth had failed to penetrate his clothing but the sensation remained and he treasured it more than the dry embrace of her hands on his. He decided to linger.

It would be a month before they met again. Manfred wondered if he would be dead by then. The blight in him was doing its work slowly but he could not be sure. If he was to die he might have wished for a more dramatic final meeting but he knew that he would never have that. He decided that he was content either way.

He lit his second cigarette of the day and reconciled himself to the cold. Another man ran past him. This man was heavier and puffed more with the strain of his labour. Manfred smiled comfortably. He sat in griefless silence, composed and ready.

SIX

(1947–50)

MANFRED returned to England that hard November. The war had changed London. The city was blistered by rubble and dust. Whole streets had disappeared and much of Manfred's old district was afflicted with holes and gaps like a set of bad teeth. Berlin had been murdered and buried by war but London limped on, wounded but hardy. Berlin had been easier to bear.

London was dotted with awkward little meetings between ex-comrades, unrecognizable in civilian clothes. Their talk was uniformly edgy and furtive. Many had failed since the end of the war. Many were bewildered and poor. They had returned to find their lives more rubbled than their homes. Jobs had disappeared or been stolen, wives had strayed or died. They were not the heroes they had expected to be. They discovered that the fruit of civilian good opinion rotted quickly. Class reasserted itself quietly. Officers with whom they had eaten, slept and shared latrines disappeared back into their differing world. The men were isolated. With a tin hat on their heads and a gun in their hands, they had forgotten how difficult their lives might again prove to be. They felt duped and betrayed. They were left with a demob suit and a cardboard case – cheap clothes for cheap people. They were home.

As in Berlin, London was host to some of those few Jews who had survived the camps and many of those who had fled Europe before the war. They were wounded Jews, cataleptic with shapeless grief. Their presence in the city was a reproach. Suicides were common. The Gentile British were slow to sympathy. All Europe had been hammered and they themselves had suffered and bled so long that the Jewish dead were lost in the crowd. The manner of the slaughter disgusted, but the *loss*, the actual reduction in living, breathing people, was almost unremarkable in the midst of the butchery.

War had hurt London but war had been won. Victory was crucial. It was a fig leaf for the city's shame and pain. When he returned home, Manfred saw how much London had lost with nothing gained. Like scores of thousands of other used-up soldiers, Manfred wandered the broken city in his cheap suit and near-paper shoes. London was penitent; shops that didn't sell, foodless cafés and empty homes. The city was piebald, mongrel. It was a dim haze of the remembered picturesque, of the death of old hope.

MANFRED found a job with a gloomy master joiner in Bethnal Green. The wages were paltry but enough for him to rent a shabby room near Petticoat Lane. His mother protested. She was angry that he did not return to live with her. She felt that the war had cost her two sons. His brother's death made Manfred's refusal to live with her even more galling. She felt betrayed and complained unjustly and bitterly of the infrequency of his visits. The more she complained, the less Manfred visited her.

He enjoyed the new work. His lugubrious employer was an instinctive and marvellous craftsman. After soldiery, Manfred found carpentry absorbing and beautiful. The smell and rub of new wood filled his days. When he went home, he washed the wood-shavings out of his hair but the citric odour of the timber remained. He learned that wood could be yielding and malleable, a blank page on which to draw. As his hands grew nimble, his mind's ease increased. The war seemed yesterday but forgotten.

His nights were various but mostly lonely. Sometimes he would drink with a few of the old battalion boys in a series of leprous bars in Whitechapel. He visited his mother and listened without love to her plaints and sorrows.

Mostly, however, he would merely walk around his neighbourhood until he was weary enough to sleep. The city's lights soothed him. Their yellow glow was ultimately civilian. Bright windows had always given him hope, man and boy. Plans would form on these walks. He would smoke a score of cut-price cigarettes and make fragile projections. Like all the men he knew, the war had slowed Manfred's life. Some of these men had just now begun the resumption of their normal lives. Manfred was slower. He continued walking the streets around his home, postponing his future night by night.

Then Tapper reappeared. After six months back in London, a letter arrived for Manfred at his mother's house. Apparently, Tapper had left Berlin under something of a cloud after some unspecified bad business with some of his American friends. His fledgling business had been smothered by the Americans and Tapper had fled Berlin soon after Manfred with bundles of dollars sewn into every garment he possessed. He was seeking new openings now for his peculiar talents. He believed that he had found the perfect scheme. He had met up with Spike and enlisted him in these new plans. He suggested a meeting with Manfred and gave his address as the Assassins on Commercial Road.

A week later, the three men met in the Assassins. Manfred was uneasy. He had already seen too many desperate reunions where men searched for the buried passions of their wartime friendships. Usually, those passions were buried deep and there remained nothing common to these men but pale stories of their shared war told with ebbing hilarity and hollow smiles.

As expected, Spike's wife had left him for his brother.

Cruelly, the family had shunned Spike because of this. They held him passively responsible. Poor Spike drank numbly as he related this. The great injustices he had always seemed to fear and invite had found him, and Spike was largely unsurprised by his misfortune. Manfred noticed that he seemed much older.

Tapper looked, if anything, more like a teenage footpad than ever. He had always been different, special, even if only especially disliked. As Tapper sat in the bar, dressed in a suit of outstanding vulgarity and poking fun at the amiable, doomed Spike, Manfred's spirits lifted. They were quickly drunk. War memories remained unswapped and they talked of the future. Tapper outlined his scheme.

London was full of refugee Jews, he said. Those who had arrived before the war were doing badly but those who had come in the past two years were drowning. These people were desperate for homes. Tapper would provide these homes. Nothing could be simpler or more lucrative.

Tapper said that it had been Manfred who had given him the idea. He had not forgotten the legion conversations in the desert when he had grilled Manfred obsessively about being a Jew. He had been hungry for details, particularly intrigued by Manfred's refusal to change his all too German, all too Jewish name even when, in war, it had proved a difficult title.

Now, Tapper said, Jews were changing their names frantically. All over London bergs and steins were being lopped off and discarded. Neutral English versions were being substituted – swathes of Greens, Browns and Whites. Jokes circulated about how many colours a Jew could be. Tapper remembered how Manfred had held fast to his one colour.

Tapper's idea was simple. He would buy houses, many houses, whole streets if possible. He would rent them to the new Jews of London. He would create his own lucrative ghettos and do the Jews a favour into the bargain.

The masterly touch in all this was that, while Jews were exploited, baited and hated, while they themselves robbed their own names of Jewishness, Tapper would do the reverse. He was going to change his name to make it *more* Jewish. He pronounced his proposed new title with pride: *Tapperstein*. Who could be more trusted by London's scarred, scared Jewry than a landlord called Tapperstein? He would seem like a redeemer. He would clean up.

Manfred was drunkenly stunned. Tapper told him and Spike that he wanted them with him. Manfred would be the frontman and rent-collector. Spike would be the handy, hard or right-hand man. With Tapper(stein)'s name, Manfred's face and Spike's muscle, they would convince and seduce. The opportunities were limitless. Tapper was amazed that no clever Jew had thought of it. The early days might be difficult but he had rescued just enough cash from Berlin to see them through.

By now, they were all very drunk indeed. Tapper let it slip that he was already running some girls out of Notting Hill. Manfred wasn't bothered by the man's pimping. He was too drunk to care. Tapper's scheme was a magical thing – preposterous but marvellous. The three men were beerily euphoric and both Manfred and Spike sottishly promised that they would work for Tapper. Then Tapper fell asleep on the table and Spike took to weeping about his wife. Having promised to be captain on Tapper's woozy ship, Manfred went home.

The next morning was purgatorial. His head was raw and dead and his flesh was infested with haggard cramps. His forearm and sleeve had been shredded by some forgotten fall and his whole body ached convulsively. Crucified by pain and remorse, Manfred washed, dressed and stumbled to work. When he got there, he was groggily astonished to find his taciturn employer in close conversation with a miraculously unhungover Tapper. When he noticed Manfred, Tapper greeted him with a wide smile and told him that he had just given Manfred's notice to the carpenter. He was in Tapper's employ now.

WITHIN a month Manfred was glad. They had bought a score of properties already and, as Tapper had predicted, they were finding tenants with ease. Tapper's eye for a purchase was sharp. He harassed the owners of any dilapidated property he saw. He cajoled them with tales of post-war depression, public housing and the imminent unsaleability of their properties. He succeeded in making them believe that he was doing them a favour. Generally, they sold quickly and gladly.

He had two basic techniques. Sometimes, he would offer a third of a house's value and still pull it off. On other occasions he would pay double what some crumbling shanty was worth. Either way, it eventually worked to his advantage. If he bought cheap, neighbouring proprietors would panic at such a fall in value and Tapper would move in and clean them out for less than they deserved. If he paid dear for one house, the other owners in *that* street would hear of the foolish price and sense an opportunity. Imagining Tapper an imbecile, they would ask his terms one after another and Tapper would pay decreasing amounts for each property.

Tapper understood that buying was easy; he knew that selling was the unstable art. Once you had nudged the idea that they might sell something into someone's mind, then any lack of sale was a failure. The increasing desire to sell could only depress the price. Tapper began to accumulate whole pockets of streets, starting by paying big prices and ending up with a row of houses for a quarter of their cumulative value. He was a genius.

Rumours that he was bringing in Jews, Negroes and

Chinese further cut the prices he had to pay. He was careful to nurture such rumours and add many of his own sensational details. For some weeks a national newspaper ran a series of doom-laden stories of a massive Chinese underworld operation opening up in Camberwell. This was based entirely on a price-dropping fantasy cooked up by Tapper while he lay drunk one night on the floor of the lounge bar in the Assassins. At one point, he was close to buying a house a day. There was no limit to his greed and no obstacle to his ambitions.

Tapper was a money poet. He understood the malleable metre of price and value. Price was a fiction to him. Nothing was worth anything until a buyer thought it so. Manfred watched him outmanoeuvre and bewilder all vendors. His vulgar suits and his floury boy's face did nothing to dent his authority. Tough sellers crumpled weakly before him. Tapper was full of the conviction that his price was the world's price. Once Tapper had valued, the price was unarguable, set for all time.

Sometimes he would not have even seen the properties which he bought. He had no further interest in them once they had been acquired. Tapper wasn't interested in property. It was buying that excited him. The act of purchase was everything. His mean little eyes would mist and redden as he bartered. His hands would tremble and he sweated oily sweat. He was almost disappointed if a sale proved *too* easy. He enjoyed his single skill.

As promised, Manfred took care of the tenants and the rents. Many of the properties were run-down and squalid but the tenants were seldom querulous. Manfred noticed that they seemed frightened of him. They were all excessively respectful and some were openly obsequious. He tried to seem sympathetic and friendly but it was a useless effort. His blandishments were simply seen as more subtle technique than the usual bluster and threats.

He dealt with families destroyed by poverty. He dreaded knocking on the doors of certain houses. There were certain constant, unchanging refrains. They would see him right next week. They didn't have it just at the moment but something was coming in soon. The excuses and flimsy pleas for extra time soon became loathsome to him. He tried to juggle the accounts so that he could allow some families a week's or a fortnight's grace. But Tapper was impatient and brutal. He counselled firmness on Manfred's part. Charity, he said, would lose all of them their jobs.

The children's plight wounded Manfred most. They all seemed shabby, underfed and cowering. He knew that many mothers threatened their children with the *Rentman*. It saddened him that he was such a bogeyman for them. The children regarded him with dread.

He soon discovered the reason for their fear. He heard rumours about Tapper's methods of dealing with rent arrears and other irritations. There was talk of summary evictions, threats, even beatings. It was no accident that the giant lumbering Gentile Spike was seen all over Tapper's properties. The tenants were terrified of Spike. Many thought that Mr Tapperstein had somehow fallen under his control. There had been some trouble early on when a rival had taken exception to Tapper(stein)'s rapid success. Tapper's grubby office windows were broken and his car damaged. There were break-ins and threats. Spike and two of his even larger friends had cleared up this difficulty violently. Again, Tapper was scrupulous in ensuring that this story circulated among his tenants: few of them risked being late with the rent. Although the threat was idle, it worked. These people had suffered so much at the hands of so many that Tapper's veiled coercion seemed almost inoffensive. There were no complaints.

Manfred was uneasy about this. But he drifted, volitionless. Tapper's energy and conviction were magnetic. Tapper knew his friend well. He maintained the fiction that Manfred didn't know about the girls he was running all over town. Both men knew that Manfred's objections were dormant if he could pretend ignorance. Manfred needed Tapper. He would drift much more dangerously if cut loose from his employer's indomitable wake. He was content to be towed Tapper's way.

Though he now earned much more, Manfred still lived in his old room at Petticoat Lane. It was still shabby and inconvenient but it lent him a kind of dispassion about the road his life had taken. At night, when back in that room, Tapper's galvanic excesses seemed remote and unreal. At home, Manfred managed to hoard his pale selfhood in the face of his employer's overwhelming dominance.

He no longer walked the neighbourhood dreaming plans. Those plans lived still but drooped sadly. Manfred felt shame at his new work. He took to lying awake at night, staring at the strange luminance of his stained ceiling. He would leave the window open and the dark air, cold or warm, would move through his room, rustling papers and sweeping dust from the shelves. His thoughts were filled with the faces of the tenants with whom he dealt. The poor, broken Jews he robbed. Pressed to his bed, room dark and window open, the city would seem to whisper to him as he lay there, to forgive, to expiate.

Six months after starting work for Tapper, Manfred met Emma. He had been collecting the rents from a clutch of houses on Hatch Street. The quality of the morning had already suffused him with optimism. The neutral, washed-out light seemed latent with promise. It was not the kind of day to spend taking money from the poor but no day was that and Manfred continued to spend them so.

When he had finished collecting from the regular houses

on the street, Manfred looked for a new one that Tapper had bought there recently. It was a tall, crumbling building whose high side faced him as he approached. At a window in that wall, he saw a young woman standing at a mirror brushing her hair. He could see little of her features but her posture and the grace of her movements were arresting. He gazed steadily, his pace slowing. He took a new rent book from his bag. When he looked up again, he was astonished to see an old woman, withered and bony, brushing her hair by the same window. The girl had disappeared as if she had never existed. The old lady glanced out of the window and found Manfred's eyes meeting hers. Manfred tipped his hat and the old woman inclined her head in a patrician manner.

When he knocked at the door, the old woman answered. When she realized that he was a rent-collector, she shepherded him into the kitchen, the obvious place for tradesmen and their like. She made tea while Manfred sat on a spindly stool, trying to explain his business. When the old woman discovered that Manfred was Jewish, her hauteur thawed a little. When he praised her tea, she became expansive.

She told him that she lived alone with her niece. The family were Czech Jews. The old lady herself had left Prague before the war but the girl and her parents had been caught there during the Occupation. The family had been wiped out. Out of two score relatives, the old woman and her niece were all that were left.

After the war, the old woman had searched without hope for surviving family members. Tracing groups had been set up by grieving British and American Jews and with the help of one of those agencies, her niece had been discovered in Berlin. She had been found living in a derelict school with a small group of women who had survived Birkenau. She was ill-fed, ill-clothed and numb. The girl had been returned to her aunt.

They had lived together now for nearly a year. The girl's health had improved and she had grown pretty. But she was silent and withdrawn. She spoke little and never of the war. The aunt had made the girl change her name from Rosza to Emma. Emma was a good English name, a name which would make it easier for the girl to find a job and perhaps even a husband. Rosza became Emma without argument and duly found a job in a haberdasher's in Camden Town.

Manfred saw nothing of the girl as the old woman spoke. He heard the soft rumbles and creaks of someone walking on wooden floors upstairs but the girl herself did not appear. He was careful to seem neutral as the old lady told him her story. He was accustomed to such stories now. Most of the people living in Tapper's houses had been damaged by the war and most of them tried to tell him about it. As though they could tell it away, could render it into memory by making it a story. Manfred had developed a habitual response – sympathetic, mystified, Hebrew. But he was rarely moved by them now. The worn women and the haunted men were too numerous to pity.

But it was different with this girl. She had appeared at the window like a girl in a fable. As he had listened to the old lady, the girl's invisibility and the history of her suffering had made her magical to him. He cared little whether, in his first brief glance, he had mistaken her beauty. He was beguiled.

Afterwards, he stood rigid on the pavement outside their home. He felt transfigured, immense. He looked up at the window in which he had seen her. No one was there. He looked at his hands and saw that they were peony red. His whole body felt flushed and scorched. He resolved that he would love the girl.

That afternoon, Manfred quizzed Tapper about his newest residents. As usual, Tapper knew infuriatingly little.

He had not seen the niece and had dealt with the old woman only briefly. He was amused to find Manfred so unsettled by a woman. Uncharacteristically, however, he did not advise Manfred to debauch the girl. He guessed that some strangeness was afoot and was dumbly pleased.

'You interested in this girl?' he asked.

'Yes.'

Tapper stubbed out his cheap cigar.

'Watch it. This kind of thing can get you married if you're not careful.'

Manfred laughed.

The following day was Sabbath. Manfred astonished his mother by visiting her. She seemed inert and quiescent. Manfred noticed that she was suddenly old. She could not have been much more than fifty but she was stooped and thin. He told her about Emma. She listened patiently, her expressionless face still. Manfred felt like a son again. Once more there was a ligament between them, the merest bond of love. He talked all day while they drank chilly tea. His mother told him that he should make the girl his.

In the months that followed, Manfred continued collecting the weekly rents, each week constructed around the visit to Emma's house. He collected the Hatch Street rents last thing on a Friday evening so that she would be home from work when he called. The old woman had taken a liking to him and he lingered as long as he could. He discovered that he had not mistaken the girl's beauty. Emma moved quietly and gracefully through the gloom of the little kitchen in which he always sat. From her toffee-coloured hair to her matt, dark eyes, she moved him. When she passed close to him, he was washed in the shield of heat that radiated from her. Near her, he jabbered like a child. Unnerved, he spoke meaninglessly of ospreys or horticulture. His enslaved gaze stuck fast to her form. When she spoke to him, he was pallid and trembling.

The old woman found him out with ease. One evening when Emma was working late, Manfred and the aunt found themselves alone. The old woman scolded him. She was weary of his procrastination. She scripted his love plan. Diffidence won nothing. She told that if he wished to court her niece, he should ask her. The old woman foresaw success. So when Emma returned, he asked her.

WITHIN a pair of months, his life was crammed with her. His days were lightless when he was not with her. His hours were spent bereft in London's murk, awash with lofty sentiment. He was exuberant and fastidious. He bought a second-hand suit and took to wearing two pairs of trousers at a time to lend bulk to his eternally thin legs. His head was clogged with lush music and his world was vermeil.

He lost himself. They were allowed little time together and were rarely alone. The aunt was censorious, prohibitive and Emma obeyed her without complaint. Mostly, the lovers would merely sit in the kitchen on the few nights he was allowed to call. Manfred would chatter blandly as the old woman clucked around them, ostentatiously leaving the room every now and then so that they might connive some chaste marriage plan. He would watch her face as he spoke. It was a grave face, shadowed but beautiful. He felt himself choked and mad with something he imagined to be love. It was a difficult commodity, as incendiary to him as an illness or an injury.

The gradient of his life steepened. He became uncharacteristic. There was a brawl in a bar over a friend's coarse comment. Manfred lost a tooth but broke a nose. He became prone to reasonless weeping. His thoughts were all pieces of love. Emma was his choicest, most precious part. Beside her, he was clumsy. He spilled his coffee on her floor, he stepped on her toes, he said foolish things. One Sunday, they went to the country north of the city. They brought wine and cold meats with them and ate in an abandoned graveyard, using the stones as tables. It rained hard and they sheltered in the porch of the broken church. He snatched a kiss as the rain dripped through the gaps in the roof. She yielded to him, bent her face to his. Her touch was velvet on his face.

THEY were married within a year. The night before the wedding, Manfred walked the city as he had used to do. He walked until dawn. The darkness deepened, shaded and gradually fled at first light. Already dressed in his wedding suit, elegant and solitary in the cold, Manfred felt like forty men. He thought of the girl he was to marry. Recently she had become a cloudy figure, obscured by the blanket of his love. That night, young Manfred had his first true presentiment of mortality. Despite his euphoria, the air seemed stamped with the temperature of death, cold head and chilly bones. Emma had never spoken of what had happened to her during the war but he knew she was filled with death. A week before, Manfred had called late at their house. Emma had been in bed. The aunt wanted her left to sleep. She busied herself in the kitchen with Manfred's request. Manfred sneaked up to the bedroom and opened the door. He looked in and saw Emma sleeping, her hand over her face, guarding her breath lest anyone steal it. He left without disturbing her and had thought then that pity, pity was most of love.

The wedding was crowded and Jewish. Men and women whom he had not seen for fifteen years were there. There were large numbers of men and women he had *never* seen. Emma's aunt had enlisted the attendance of a regiment of sentimental matrons and everyone that Manfred's mother had ever met was there. Tapper was hugely in evidence, flattered to be invited to such a Jewish occasion. He had obviously done his homework and could be heard singing Hatikvah to astonished guests at any available opportunity. Manfred had to spend thirty minutes dissuading him from trying to impress the rabbi with his knowledge of Scripture.

The day was bright and the cut of the sun sliced rooms and people into glittering segments like photographs of some recent past. Emma was pale and heartbreaking. They stood underneath the wedding canopy, deaf to the rabbi's mumbled exhortations. The canopy filtered the gleam of sunlight into an improbable, hope-filled glow. It seemed to Manfred to be asking for trouble. He hoped that the optimistic cloth above them would oversee their marriage as it should. He hoped it would cast no shadow.

SEVEN

BIRDS twittered and chirped outside Manfred's bathroom window as he defecated, giving the business, he thought, an elusive and unaccustomed pastoral air. The toilet seat was by now glissome and sheer with his sweat. He wiped his face with some toilet paper. His panic seemed to have concluded for now. The holocaust in his bowels had subsided. His rectum felt baked and livid as though he had been voiding molten lava or titanium rods.

Neither constipation nor its reverse, Manfred's last twenty minutes had been as gasping and impossible as a monstrous birth. His flesh had dilated beyond nature and he had wept with pain and shame. His decline was truly marching now. Over the past week his bathroom walls had viewed calmly as he grunted and gnashed through his pop-eyed toilet. Three days before there had been blood among the stools and much of it. Good blood, good viscous blood, bright and vital. He had stopped looking now.

As he wiped himself, Manfred wondered precisely what these new developments augured. He knew little about colonic integrity but he imagined that crapping such prodigious gore was a very final step. Also, he was feeling increasingly terrible after these defecations. For an hour or more his innards would feel traumatized or indignant as though they had been roughly shaved with a blunt razor.

Indeed, as he stood and pulled his trousers over his withered hips, something integral seemed to have happened to his spine. His back felt scorched and rigid as though a corset of steel had embedded itself in his flesh. He felt giddy and nauseous.

A pot of coffee awaited him in his kitchen. He poured some and sat himself very gingerly on the softest chair in his sitting room. As always, the coffee soothed and he felt once more that it was a fine thing to be dying. His toilet troubles were a sure sign – though he hoped that he would not have the misfortune to die there. In Libya a lugubrious Welsh corporal had shot himself famously in the latrines and had been discovered face down in the shit pit. This circumstance had robbed the man's suicide of any tragedy and had been a favourite battalion joke for some months. Though Manfred was not proud, he did not want any lavatorial absurdity spoiling the dignity of his final moment.

An hour had passed since he had struggled into the bathroom and Martin would arrive soon. A disastrous crap like that was not the best way to prepare for the multiple irritations of one of his son's visits. The old man hoped fervently that Martin would not bring Julia. Manfred detested his daughter-in-law. He was conscious that Martin had many grievances and hidden hatreds concerning his childhood. He knew that his son considered him the poor father. Julia was Martin's revenge upon his father. The precision of his choice could only have been intentional. Julia was a constant, indefatigable goad.

They had just spent the weekend with Emma. This made their visit doubly unwelcome. Manfred was always testier than usual when they had recently seen his wife. Their access to her was a reproach and the laborious tact with which Julia would not mention Emma at such times was a poor concealment of her triumph. It nauseated him. He had no proof of how much his daughter-in-law knew of his own ruined marriage but he imagined that it was nearly all. Emma liked her, he knew. He wondered how much the woman had been told and how much she had guessed for herself (she was bright enough in such things and prided herself on such sensitivity).

They had proposed taking him out for lunch in one of Martin's favourite restaurants. Manfred burned with resentment. This, he supposed, was some form of consolation after their visit to Emma. A palliative to keep him sweet. It was an insult to his decrepitude that it was now his son who took *him* out for afternoon treats. Manfred promised himself that he would make the afternoon as unpleasant as possible for them.

THEY arrived, hardly punctual as usual. Martin looked as implacably vigorous as ever and, to the old man's irritation, Julia was flushed and pretty. Her hair was disordered and her skirt uncharacteristically creased. Manfred wondered if they had just made love. Such ardour from his healthy, lumpen son seemed unlikely. Not, he conceded, that Julia did not merit such passion. Despite his great dislike for her, the old man could not deny his daughter-in-law's charms.

'You look pale, Manfred,' she murmured as she kissed his cheek. Manfred sniffed for any stray ruttish odours but only caught the mild fragrance of her elegant neck.

He mumbled something neutral and shuffled towards his son's outstretched hand. Already his gambit had been chosen. His gait was embarrassingly frail. He would repay their largesse with pantomimic elderliness. He almost winced at his son's exemplary handshake and lowered himself into his armchair with infinite labour. Martin slipped his hand into his pocket and looked foolish.

(Martin had started shaking hands with his father just after his marriage to Julia. It was an attempt at a manly gesture but it was also a gesture without respect or benevolence. The old man knew that the studied formality of this greeting was another attempt at distance, an insult. The first time it had happened both men had blushed in acknowledgement of the snub but now it was an old taunt empty of meaning.)

Julia's hand strayed through her hair, tugging its dark abundance. She sat down and looked appraisingly at her husband's father. 'Have you been ill again?' she asked.

Manfred glanced at his son, who remained standing, his gaze wandering towards Manfred's bedroom. This irritated the old man unaccountably. He answered Julia. 'Well, you know, just the usual trials. Spending hours on the toilet.' He saw Martin's face wrinkle with distaste and pressed on, 'It's not that I'm constipated, you understand. I'm pooping punctually enough.' He smiled innocently. 'Yes, I'm certainly shitting on schedule.'

Julia muttered something incomprehensible but sympathetic and encouraging in equal measure. He saw her blush again. He suspected that she knew he wanted trouble. She glanced quickly (too quickly) at her husband. Martin started clumsily.

'Do you mind if we have a cup of coffee before we leave?' he asked his father. Manfred nodded silently and Martin trudged guiltily into the kitchen.

The ruse was clumsy and obvious, so prearranged that Manfred wanted to laugh. They had something to tell him before they took him out to lunch. Something that they pompously considered of too much moment to be unveiled in a common restaurant. Even Manfred was surprised at how little intrigued he was.

'We thought we might have some coffee and a little chat before we went out.' The tact in her voice annoyed the old man. He wondered what forbearance or diplomacy made this woman speak to him with such overwhelming sensitivity. She seemed almost proud of being able to speak to him at all. What disgust had she overcome? How much had

Martin told her of his childhood, of Manfred's own motley fatherhood and husbandship?

His silence compelled Julia to speak again. 'There's something we wanted to tell you about.' They could both hear gauche noise from the kitchen as Martin prepared the coffee. 'Martin has wanted to tell you for some time but I wanted to be absolutely sure before we told you.'

Despite her tact, despite her great care, a blush of triumph suffused her face and Manfred knew. Her expression made it clear. He knew.

He puffed and spluttered, winded by the shock of his grief. Sudden hatred made his gut bubble. He was amazed by the extent of his rage and fear. Now he understood Julia's overbearing gentleness and that flush she could not conceal. His indignation choked his throat tight. He had not known how much their childlessness had comforted him until now.

'Manfred?'

He grew conscious that Julia was watching him and that his traitor face was betraying all his shame. He struggled to compose himself. He looked at her. She even *looked* fertilized. Languorous and replete. The long shame of her barrenness had disappeared. Those marks on her face had fled completely overnight.

'You've guessed, haven't you?' she said.

Unable to master his voice, Manfred nodded.

'We were only sure last week,' Julia continued, her blushing coquetry fading as she saw his unmistakable horror. 'Like I say, Martin wanted to tell you before but I wanted to be sure. I hope I did the right thing.' She frowned. Her voice was authoritative. Manfred knew that she had found him out. She glanced towards the kitchen. Martin had nearly finished his business there. Julia was giving the old man a chance to prepare himself for his son's return. Martin need not know of his father's first reaction. In some way that

Manfred could not define, Julia was promising to keep his horror secret.

With untypically good timing, Martin returned. He sat down beside Julia and took one of her hands in his. His eyes met his father's. He did not seem surprised at the old man's consternation. He obviously considered it natural. His own face was more open and eager than Manfred thought he had ever seen it. There was a long nervous silence as they waited for Manfred to say something. The old man gulped, his face pale.

'Congratulations to you both.' The smile he tried, trembled and flagged. 'It came as a surprise,' he glanced at Julia's impassive face, 'but I'm very glad for you both.' His smile returned with more confidence.

Galvanized by this, Martin lurched from his seat and approached his father, his hand held out again. Embarrassed, Manfred offered his own and his son grasped it double-handed. Martin's eyes were moist as he shook his father's hand and his cheeks oscillated slightly with the vehemence of his exertion. Julia, too, had risen and come to Manfred's other side. She took the old man's other hand and laughed and sobbed. Manfred, still seated, with both their hands in his, felt like a bogus patriarch.

Such emotion had not been executed with enough confidence to last for long and Julia and Martin soon returned to their sofa. Martin looked foolish. He smiled weakly at Manfred and said, 'Julia's due next February. If it's a boy we were thinking of calling him Manfred.' He paused, waiting for his father's joyful thanks.

'Oh, I don't think you should do that,' said Manfred.

'Oh. Why not? We thought you'd be pleased.' Martin's tone was hurt.

'Well, yes, I'm pleased that you thought of it but you can't call a child Manfred any more. It's an old name. It's a dead name.'

'Manfred!' Julia squealed. 'That's a terrible thing to say. It's not a dead name. It's your name.'

Manfred smiled at her and changed the subject. 'Does your mother know?' he asked Martin.

Martin's face grew evasive and comically guilty, like an apprehended boy.

'Yes. We . . . ah . . . we told her at the weekend. It was pure chance that we saw her before you.'

He should not have added the second remark. Manfred accepted Emma's right to know first. He had not minded that she had been the first to be informed of such news, so unwelcome to him. But Martin's consolatory waffle about pure chance enraged him. He did not like to be pitied so openly. He rose from his armchair and announced that the coffee would be ready. He strode into the kitchen in a feeble sulk.

His hands shook as he gathered cups. He could hear their lowered voices from the other room. His belly was fevered and raw with pain. His bowels felt abrasive and caustic. He had seen Emma since Martin and Julia had visited her. Or rather, he smiled bitterly, he had *met* Emma since then. She had already known that Julia was pregnant and yet she had not told him. He felt cowed and broken by the multiple injustices of his life.

'Can I help?'

Martin had followed him into the kitchen, obviously instructed by his wife. She did not want to give Manfred any time to fulminate alone in the kitchen. The old man looked bitterly at his son. Martin looked sheepish and upset. Manfred pointed mutely at the coffee pot. Martin picked it up and moved towards the sitting room. He paused at the door. He looked back at his father.

'Be happy for us,' he said sadly. 'We've waited a long time. Try to be happy for us.'

Manfred filled a tray with cups, saucers, sugar and milk. He picked it up and tried to smile at his son.

'The coffee will get cold,' he said.

THEY did not go out for lunch. They negotiated a delicate hour over their coffee cups. Manfred tried to be glad for them. It was a poor effort. He had watched their faces darken at his reaction. Julia did her best to maintain some peace but Martin grew duller and more mutinous by the minute. They were close to an open fight when Webb arrived. Manfred's neighbour had unwittingly saved the day. Unbothered by Manfred's guests, he had made himself quite comfortable beside Julia on the sofa. Within minutes he was making some woozy attempt at seducing his neighbour's daughter-in-law. Although it was barely midday, he was quite drunk. For one terrifying period he seemed to be considering the possibility of picking a fight with Martin whom he obviously considered a wimp and a bore.

But when he discovered that Julia was pregnant both his pugilism and his lechery vanished. He was grotesquely, drunkenly pleased. He kissed both Julia *and* Martin and could not be prevented from scurrying back to his flat and producing a bottle of whisky from which he forced them all to drink. His glee, though only the promiscuous benevolence of the drunk, shamed Manfred. Julia was genially indulgent with Webb's grand congratulations and even Martin became tolerant. His cheeks flushed red from the whisky and Webb's admiration of his manhood. Manfred knew that he should have mustered an approximation of Webb's gross enthusiasm. And as Martin and Julia ineffectually fielded Webb's slobbering delight, he knew that they thought so too. He was merely glad, however, that his neighbour had so effectively substituted for him. At least their news had been marked in some way.

They had all waited for Webb to leave but Webb's oblivion was impermeable. After an hour, the whisky bottle was nearly empty and Webb had fallen sonorously asleep. Martin was woozy with drink and satisfaction. Julia shepherded him into the bathroom like a child and made him wash his face with cold water. While her husband was in the bathroom she asked for one of Manfred's cigarettes and smoked furtively.

'You take it when he comes out. Now I'm pregnant, he'd hit the roof if he saw me smoking.' Manfred was not seduced by the intimacy of this confession. He acquiesced blankly and Julia frowned. Webb vented a particularly brutish snore and they both glanced at him. Julia's tone became brisk.

'I know it's difficult for you, Manfred, and I know you'll come round. You'll have a grandchild. That must please you.'

Manfred inclined his head without comment.

Julia continued, proofed against his frost. 'I don't know what it is with you, Manfred, but soon I'll be past caring. You're not going to ruin this for me. Or for Martin. We've waited too long. We're going to be happy in spite of you.'

In the bathroom, a toilet flushed and the sound of water in the basin was clear. She hesitated, perhaps surprised and sorry at the tone she had taken. She looked at Manfred with something close to pity.

'You know, Emma told me not to tell you about the baby. She said that it wouldn't matter much in a couple of months.' She paused. 'She told me that you wouldn't be pleased. She wouldn't tell me why and I didn't believe her but she was right, wasn't she?'

'No, she wasn't,' Manfred lied.

They had left soon afterwards and Manfred had been glad to see them go. Webb slept on for an hour or so and Manfred sat watching him, smoking and drinking some of the little that was left of his neighbour's whisky. Webb flinched and yelped through his slumber like an old dog. The man seemed to be making a habit of falling asleep in Manfred's flat. It was an almost laudable instance of his great ease. When he finally woke he was full of absurd dignity. He congratulated Manfred again on his imminent grandchild. Martin was something of a geek, he said, but the girl was a piece of class. Still, a grandchild was a grandchild. The bloodlines would continue or something like that. Gathering the whisky bottle, Webb left.

The rest of the day was thick time, heavy and particular. Manfred watched his windows dim and darken as the day grew late. When he lit the lamps, he left the curtains open and stared at the reflection of his lighted self and room in the black sheen of his window. Such window images of his night-time room always depressed him. The objects in his life, the old furniture and cheap carpets, the almost bare walls, the litter of unread books and his own shabby reflection, it all seemed even more squalid when seen back to front in dark glass. His spirits sank and he closed the curtains.

Martin and Julia had been married for more than ten years and had been trying to have a child for over half that time. Their failure after the first two years became onerous and unspoken. Julia suffered in particular. After each of them had been inspected, smeared and sampled, it was discovered that Julia was infertile. She had been devastated. She felt herself to be faulty. Manfred did not discourage this idea and even dropped some blameless hints to his son about the perils of marrying Gentile women. In the secret part of himself that he reserved for his smallest hatreds and envy, Manfred was pleased that she was barren. It seemed just. If his son had started producing leagues of children, the old man would have felt himself even more obsolete. The lack in their life had comforted him obscurely. It had eased the lack in his own.

Their news had wounded and diminished him like a loss, like the unexpected success of friend or enemy. It was like a blow that they had intended. Indeed, Julia's caution proved that she knew he would take it hard. It was an act of defiance. His son had superseded him (as always) in some crucial way. He felt thwarted and desperate.

He tried to sleep but couldn't. As he churned under the hot, heavy blankets, his chest was electric with pain. After an hour or so, he was hot and wet with sweat and ache. When he struggled out of bed, he looked back at the disordered sheets and saw that they were damp and stained with his sweat.

He sat in the bathroom and smoked the last of the cigarettes. The twisting of his gut grew steady and persistent. He could bear such pain with fortitude now. His abdomen felt culled, reduced. He thought of his son. Martin was not yet forty and already he was inflating into gross middle age. Children were supposed to be the parents' past made flesh. They were supposed to stop it being necrotic. They were supposed to be the living past. The old man wondered how much his strange separation from his wife had made Martin what he was. Negotiating the neutrality of the divided child had doubtless helped to make him moderate in his habits. Manfred felt sorry for him.

But now Martin would have a child. As the night grew cold and old, Manfred found himself almost glad. He hoped it would be a daughter. Emma deserved to have a trace of herself handed on to the world. A heartbreaking simulacrum. Manfred was glad that he would never see the child. Son or daughter, he was glad of that.

By the time Manfred had smoked his last cigarette the bathroom had grown glossy with light. He stood up and opened the window without hope. To his surprise, fresh air rinsed his face, bringing the exterior and its life to him. It had rained overnight and he had to squint at the colourless gilt of the wet streets. He smelt the special smell of the early hours of the morning; a breadsmell, overwhelmingly matutinal. The smell of readiness.

EIGHT

(1951-6)

THEIR first two years were breathless. Manfred was surprised to find himself married. He was surprised to find himself married to Emma. It was odd to find his future so joyously countermanded. His life changed. It became geared for her as hers was for him. The duty elated him, a small golden obligation. But he was still surprised.

He found himself in receipt of something he could scarcely bear. Naked, her beauty was insupportable. He whined as if in pain. The slope of her breasts, the silver incline of her belly. He was speechless, stung by the geometry of her, by her peerless skin and the sense of grace deep and shallow in her flesh. An idea of beauty that the war had killed in him was reborn.

For the first two years they lived in an apartment close to Manfred's old one. Manfred made a deal with Tapper, who had recently bought a house on Canonbury Street for a tiny sum. Manfred wanted to buy it from his employer. Tapper had already installed tenants. In two years, the rent these tenants paid would have covered half of Tapper's original price. If Manfred could match the other half in two years, the house would be his. Manfred knew that Tapper was lying and that the cumulative sum from this transaction would come to half again what Tapper had paid for the house but he realized that for Tapper this was close to largesse.

Manfred toiled obsessively. If work was all that was needed to give Emma a home, it seemed an easy thing. He began study for clerical exams. Such a qualification would make him more useful to Tapper, whose business continued to expand. In addition, if Tapper's dodgy commercial edifice finally fell apart, Manfred would find it easier to get another job.

Emma continued working at the haberdasher's. Her hours were long and arduous but she was uncomplaining. Their time together was brief but precious. Saving all they could to pay for their future house, those first two years were lived out in almost Bohemian squalor – piano, cat and portrait. The rooms smelt of bacon and coal, the walls were dingy with age and unwashable dirt. Their days began at 6 a.m., Emma sitting in her dressing gown in front of the fire she had just lit, one coaly hand held out in front of her as if wet. Manfred sat behind the table, studying profit and loss for two hours before work, his eyes sore and filmy with sleep.

But Emma's robe would flap open, her legs would stretch on the rug or her face would turn towards him in a certain attitude and Manfred would leave his papers and come to her on the floor. In the changing light of early day, he found new aspects of her, hidden corners and other stretches of flesh to cherish.

Work was two years of chilly mornings and breakfast in the first-floor office when Emma still lingered in his nostrils. He would stare open-mouthed at the patterns in Tapper's frosted glass, oblivious to the gossip of Alice, Tapper's badly paid but loquacious secretary. He listened happily to tenants' grievances, his thoughts elsewhere, an uxorious smile on his face. Tapper complained that he was sometimes abstracted but he didn't seem to care much. Little could disrupt Tapper's self-absorption.

She was easy to love. His desire was overwhelming. Her clothes, loose or taut, incited him to touch. Her buttocks swelled under his hands. He watched the shapes and gradients of muscle that lay under the flesh of her belly, rib to hip. Her breasts were like bread. Sometimes, at night, she would lie on the rug in front of the fire, her back facing him, her naked spine curving in a gentle parabola. In the dim light, she was the colour of sand or certain dead leaves.

He nagged her to feel pride in this beauty. He would urge her to look at her nakedness in the glass. The neutral, incomprehending gaze with which she beheld herself frustrated him. No tribute to her beauty seemed to move her. Her glance at the glass told her little and though the contact between their skin more than tingled, his desire could not make her vain.

But she too was ardent, immodest for the times. There were frenzied mornings when she woke wild with remorse, having killed him in her dreams. She pressed herself to him, leaving sticky trails on his skin. She pushed her nipples into his mouth, hard gems on her breasts. Once, in their first summer, they lay in bed eating peaches. Emma ate two and handed her half-eaten third to Manfred. She pulled her clothing apart and pushed her pelvis towards him, proffering herself. He pulled the stone from the peach's dripping flesh and moved that flesh towards her, gently touching her very middle. The smell was the extraordinary thing. As the fruit was rubbed away against her, the heat of her body filled the room with peach smells, drowsy and slow. In the end only the furry skin of fruit was left in his hands and the warm trails on her legs which had dried and melted again.

It seemed so much more than he could justly expect. With her, life seemed limitless and impossible. He could happily imagine a score of years merely listening to her sing or watching her rest her chin on her hand. The happiness she promised him seemed biddable and reckless. He could not imagine it spoiling. He could not imagine its ruin. That worried him.

★

ON 14 June 1952, Manfred and Emma moved into the house they owned. That day, Manfred felt like a solid man. As Emma unpacked their belongings, he wandered through the empty, bare rooms and breathed the air of ownership. He felt taller and stronger. He could scarcely believe that the house was theirs, that it would not go away. It was a building, an edifice of brick, slate, wood and glass. Nothing could be more substantial. He was proud of what he had given her. He stood by a window and pressed his hand against the wall; it felt firm and flat, it felt heavy as love.

As the day grew dim, he interrupted her unpacking and stood her by the window. Though impatient to unpack, she was tolerant and amused. He told her that the house was hers. He gave it to her proudly without hope of thanks. This, he told her, was what he wanted to do for her. This was the way he wanted to love her.

That night they slept on a pile of blankets laid across the floor. After a few sleepless hours, he kissed her awake and they made love silently on that unyielding bed. He was too proud to sleep and too excited to allow her to sleep. They talked till dawn and then dozed fitfully as sunlight streamed through the uncurtained windows. He woke late to the distant sound of Emma singing as she made breakfast. The song was some Czech rhyme. The noise of her singing, the long sunlight in the empty bedroom and the fragrance of toast throughout the house filled him with glee. He dressed and rose.

The house was the second last in a tall terrace on Canonbury Street. It was barely fifty yards from New River Walk, a tiny sliver of park, never more than a street wide, that ran from Islington to Highbury. A wide stream ran through the crazy little park and sometimes there was barely room to walk the path between river and railings. Manfred loved its absurdity. He liked to walk there with Emma in the evenings, stepping over the ducks and peeping into the bright kitchens of the elegant houses on each side.

He worked hard to pay Tapper the balance of the price. Every extra hour or day he worked was easy effort. The notion of Emma and Emma's house was wind in his sails. The idea of returning home to her at the end of the day also made his industry no labour. He would watch the clock in the frosty little office, watch the minute hand shake its fists at him. The time he spent at work became increasingly disposable time, a qualification or apprenticeship for the real time that he would spend with her.

She, too, worked harder. The haberdasher's had grown to a department store. Sometimes she worked late and he was home first. Without her, the house would seem meaningless, a strived-for folly. He would light the lamps and take much time to cook a meal for her. Absurdly, he would feel as bereft as an abandoned child. When she returned, his greeting would be effusive. He would take her coat and shoes and seat her at the table where her meal already lay. If she was weary or drawn, he would be disappointed and hurt. Kindly, she would summon some brightness into her face and manner. She would ease his mood with some complaint about a colleague or a customer and he would happily be annoyed on her behalf.

On special nights, they went to a club near Charing Cross. She would wear her best dress, a half-price staff bargain from the store in which she worked. Despite her cheap dress and uncoiffured hair, she was marvellous, bewildering the men and women both. He loved the little club and the pride he felt in this beautiful wife. They danced softly or watched the other dancers patrolling the floor clumsy and tender as elephants.

They went there with the Rosens. Manfred had known Tom Rosen at school. They met again because Tom's wife, Sarah, worked in Emma's shop. They all grew close. Those nights were always festive and happy. Sarah, too, was beautiful, sloe eyes and mesmeric hips. Tom called her Chestnut Bob on account of her hair, which was thick and splendid like Emma's. This passed for a witticism with Tom. Both men liked watching their wives together. They seemed companion pieces, complementary and entire. The independence of their talk and laughter beguiled the men. They liked how little they were needed when their wives were together.

There were nights when she seemed pictured there. Bright against the dark and smoke, small gestures she made would be much of what he remembered about her in later years. She would wipe a strand of damp hair from her forehead and lean closer to Sarah while she laughed. A piece of jewellery would glint on the soft breast of her dress. She would pull her short jacket across her naked shoulders and lift her glass simultaneously, a smile ready to press itself on her lips. She would turn in her chair to call a waiter and her hand would trail and rest on Sarah's shoulder.

And on all the nights in all the years they went there, his pleasure in the club was doubled by the thought of their leaving and going home to the house he had built for her. When they were out, the house seemed even more beautiful and astounding. Then its allure was latent, expected and therefore sharper. The leaving was almost best. After the smoke and noise of the club, the wide air was clean and silent. They would walk to Cambridge Circus to look for cabs. When wet, the streets shone like metal and the night would feel metropolitan and glamorous. He would watch Emma as she walked with her friend, her heels clicking like a clock and he would long to love her there on the street.

When they got home, dawn would be a rumour in the air and the soft music of the club would linger in his mind. They would make tired, slow love that felt like cigarettes or jazz, then sleep late and happy. There were a hundred such nights, each one long and dark and comely. They were what he had married for.

And he worked on the house. Traces of the skills he had learned from the glum carpenter in Bethnal Green remained and he worked obsessively. He built shelves and cupboards. He built tables and dressers. He built chairs, doors, wardrobes and drawers. He worked with rich wood, dark and light. His hands grew rough and hard. In his grasp, the lumber was firm and warm. It, too, felt like love.

Every morning as he left for work, he paused outside the front door. He ran his hand over the brickwork around the door, wet or dry, warm or cold. He would marvel at the thought that these bricks belonged to him. Or to her. It added inches to his stature and a foot or more to his stride. It had some intelligible reality that made him feel a full man for almost the first time that he could remember. All the other Manfreds had been early Manfred, practice Manfred. He was coming to some true version of himself, monogamous, home-owning.

His mother died before they had been in the house a year. She was barely sixty. For six months she had withered and dwindled like a fruit squeezed dry. She was buried on a pale weekday. Tapper and Spike closed the office and accompanied him to the funeral. Emma clasped his hand in hers. They were the only mourners. As they stood over his mother's boxed body, Manfred struggled to grieve. He tried to summon some poignant picture of the dead woman but could only remember the hot day when he had seen her naked.

His brother had not come to see her buried. He lived in America. He had written to Manfred asking him to see that she was buried decently and excusing himself because of some dire emergency in his business. Manfred was sad that he, her least-loved son, was the son that buried her. He never communicated with his brother again.

That night, he decided he wanted – he needed – a child. He was tired of being childless – not knowing the influence of unreturned love. Emma was quiet and sympathetic, expecting him to grieve for his dead mother. He pulled her into bed and surprised her by the exuberance of his unprotected love. He felt a milder desire, a fertile desire. A month before, she had spoken of children and now as he remained in her, she knew what he attempted. It was fortunate that she agreed and held him tight to her.

Martin was conceived that night. When she discovered she was pregnant, Manfred waited impatiently for her belly to grow. Months seemed to pass without any discernible difference. Then the skin over her womb tautened and began to swell. He was intoxicated, entirely absorbed by her. Her skin darkened on her belly and breasts. She became like another, discrete woman and his lust trebled.

And the house, too, seemed to grow in readiness for its new occupant. With a home, a lifelong career and a pregnant wife, Manfred began to feel himself a parody of domesticity. There were times, guilty moments, when he wondered if this life, this marriage-happiness, was all. He knew that it might seem a small result but he was always content with that. There was enough – there was much in this small result. The war had made him capable of happiness with little. With Emma he had found more than he had expected or deserved. Emma's pregnancy had changed him. He felt thankfully less manly, less soldier. The new impositions on his time and habits did not bother him. They were faithful bonds and he did not chafe under them.

It was a hopeful time for them when all seemed possible. Manfred even started to think himself handsome. He had decided that fatherhood would become him. That winter, London was the colour of tin. It stayed cold and he banked the fires throughout the house and made her sit close. The warmths they found were various but joint. In bed they lay long, he warmed her, he steeped her in his flesh, his clay. When she slept, he tortured himself with thoughts of her death (their death), of waking up to find her cold beside him. He feared that. The unappealable loss. He entertained himself nightly with tender thoughts of her dying.

Her pregnancy was nights spent gauging the placid weight of her breasts. The shadow he cast over her as he stood beside her chair, solicitous, enquiring. A kitchen filled with the smell of his cooking, onions, vetch and beans. Afternoons when he walked in the narrow chilly park while she slept, swollen and warm in their bed. Mornings when he shined her shoes as he sat on the end of the bed by her feet. Her silences and small moods. Her nausea and exhaustion. Her naps and dozes when her mouth fell open and she drooled but prettily.

Near the end she slept most of the day and when he was not at work, he found himself unoccupied. He could do no work in the house lest he wake her and, for once, enforced idleness in the house he loved was onerous. He took to spending time in the museum. He loved its silence and cool space. He chiefly liked the statuary. Its coolness, its beauty reminded him of what he wanted his family to be. There were many images of mother and child, of nudity, stolid, massive, cold and lovely. He saw Emma in undraped terracotta women and felt himself to be one of the men, an emblem of a marble cavalier, smooth and perfect. He longed to touch them, to feel the hard bite of the Negro stone.

The museum itself was as important as what it housed. He loved it like he loved his home. Colonnades, courtyards, pilasters and capitals. A discreet public life, hushed, sensual, eternal. He sat or walked there for hours. It lent him appetite. It made him hungry and thirsty, both. There he felt himself a paragon of sentience, warm flesh to cold stone. He felt fecund and substantial in the sterile widths of the great building. And when he returned to his childbearing wife, a trace of the museum's nobility would linger in the sight of her, quiet and full.

She gave birth to their son on a late March Sabbath. After a nine-hour labour he did not share, a young midwife admitted him to Emma's bedside. The room in which she lay was dull – custard-coloured walls and grimy blue curtains on a small window. Emma was a crumpled shape on the bed and, myopic with anxiety, Manfred stood uselessly for some moments until another woman handed him a small red thing in a towel. The bloody face was creased and irate. As he looked at this son, this child, he felt superfluous. He smiled clumsily.

But when Emma returned home a few days later, he had cleared, painted and furnished a nursery for the child. His love for it felt strongest when he worked wood and painted walls for it. In a flush of benevolence Tapper had allowed him a month off work. Tapper and Spike had both visited Emma in hospital. Poor Spike had wept weakly when he saw the child and Manfred had been stirred to tenderness and pride.

For weeks, Manfred was too stunned to think. He could only watch as Emma sustained the baby. He liked to watch the child feeding, though sometimes he felt queasy jealousy as the little thing sucked her breast. He marvelled at the child's skill. The little hand lay expertly under the breast and around the other side, squeezing intermittently, coaxing. It sucked irregularly, seeming to pause for breath or ingestion. Pause. Suck. Pause. Suck. Doubtless all babies had this skill but to Manfred it seemed an idiosyncrasy peculiar to his son. It seemed ominous, precocious and dominant.

They named the child Martin. Tom and Sarah Rosen were constant callers in Canonbury Street. They no longer spent their Friday nights at the little club. Though neither Tom nor Sarah was orthodox, they seemed to think that the child should be brought up fully Jewish. Privately, Tom and Manfred had discussed the boy's circumcision. Manfred wanted a doctor and Tom thought it was best to go to a mohel. In such a matter, he said, tradition was no cost. A mohel would do no harm.

Manfred had been remote from the troublesome society of other Jews for a long time. His father had been the only provider of Judaism. He could still remember dull, frightened afternoons with the old man. The children of Israel, he had praised, surrounded by cats and Scripture. When young, Manfred had imagined God to be a man like his father. Frail, enraged and afraid of the dark. In Scripture, night was fear. He had confused his mother's lack of faith with her defiance of his father and this witnessed apostasy had made it impossible to be godly. He might believe in but he could never love a man he imagined to be like his father. When his father died, Manfred didn't want a God, Jewish or Gentile. He had had enough of that Grand Man and his savage blessings.

Emma said nothing. She never talked about being a Jew. Occasionally, she might describe someone as Gentile but apart from that one might barely have known that she was a Jew. She observed no faith. She never spoke any Yiddish or Hebrew (all the apostate Jews Manfred had ever known had laced their talk with Yiddish and Hebrew, as though it was irony or wit). Their marriage had been Jewish but they had never observed a Sabbath or Passover. Emma spoke little of her parents and Manfred had never found the courage to ask her about what had happened to her in the camps. Her Jewishness was invisible. He took it on faith.

In the end, the boy *was* circumcised by a mohel. Manfred was never really sure why he had given in. The compromise was a symptom of the unease with which he had moved into fatherhood. He and Tom Rosen attended the ceremony (Tapper had been desperate to come, too, but Manfred had baulked at this – Tapper's fake Jewishness was becoming unhealthy, he thought). The mohel was a grimy little man whose false teeth clicked and rattled when he spoke. The child cried lustily when he beheld this figure and when his penis was cut, he screamed with outrage and injury. The mohel chuckled some loose-toothed joke and Manfred smiled uncertainly as his son was handed back to him. Tom shook his hand and he blushed.

Afterwards, the mohel had tried to sell Manfred some stones for his son, some red jasper which would bring the boy health and wisdom. The man's teeth clacked rapidly as he proffered the jewels in his greasy hands. He claimed that it was traditional. All good Jewish fathers bought stones for their sons at such times. Despite the loose dentures, the mohel's smile was professional. Still holding his screaming son, Manfred gave the man some money.

When he brought child and stones home, he hid the jasper in the drawer of the desk where he sometimes worked. He was ashamed of his purchase, the jasper seemed a poor talisman, a superstition. Tom laughed when he heard what Manfred had done. He told his friend that the mohel had obviously figured him for an apostate and tricked him, realizing that he would mystify Manfred with any old rubbish he happened to be carrying. The idea of the lucky jasper was a gull.

Manfred was sure that this was true. But his anger did nothing to lessen his unease about the stones. The banality of the trick made them seem even more grotesque. He almost blamed the child. He had been duped on his account. The discomfort he felt when with the child was increased by this episode. When Emma placed the infant in his arms, he could barely conceal his distaste.

A fortnight after the guilty circumcision, he took the loathed jasper from the drawer and, on his way to work, surreptitiously dropped them into the narrow canal of the little park beside his house. That day, he breathed easier but when, that night, he tried to hold his son with confidence, the boy still felt alien and disturbing. He handed the child back to his mother.

Despite his disappointment with the child, he still liked to watch them together. If anything, Emma seemed more beautiful when she was with the boy. In his tininess, his plump wrinkled ugliness, he was a foil to her. If he loved the child, he loved it for its mother. He told no one of this. He was ashamed. Others, the Rosens, Tapper and Spike, thought him a good father. Only Emma knew that something had changed in him. But she must have thought it temporary. She said nothing. Perhaps she hoped that, in time, he would grow more comfortable or that the extent of her own love for the boy would move him.

But when Manfred had gone back to work, he realized that he was jealous of the child. Her love for the thing was so massive and tangible that he could feel it separating them physically when they slept. If the child itself had been bodily between them, it could not have been a more substantial impediment. Emma could only have less time for her husband now that she had this greedy child to sustain. Manfred could no longer bear to watch as the infant sucked at her breast; the cheeks puffing and sucking at her nipple enraged him. Its little hand around her breast. The appetite was urgent and gross. It seemed sensual.

He could hardly bear to go to work now. He hated leaving them alone in the house together. He began to wish that they had had a daughter. Emma deserved a daughter. He himself could have loved a daughter with ease. He knew that his antagonism was obscene and ridiculous but he could not surrender his jealousy. He advised Emma to wean the child early. He rehearsed for her theories of rigorous child-care. Breastfeeding a child too long was degenerate and unwise. He even searched bookshops for childcare books which endorsed this theory. When he found one, he presented it to her with self-righteous triumph, only barely disgusted with himself.

She weaned the child before he was four months old. For two weeks, Martin squalled and screamed. The house was a nightmare of noise and infant grief. Manfred felt that the child knew what had happened and that it hated him for it. Manfred and Emma made love again. He paid particular attention to her breasts, he kissed and stroked them, sucking her nipples before she had properly finished lactating. One night he found milk in his mouth. For the first time in their marriage, Emma asked him to stop. Manfred was humiliated and angry. He felt ashamed, caught-out. And again, the child seemed to have been given precedence. But he stopped none the less.

It was easier after the child was weaned. Much of Manfred's jealousy faded or lost its venal edge. He even managed a proprietorial affection for the boy. The child, too, seemed calmer after his rage at being denied her breast. An uneasy, fragile truce was conducted between the father and infant son.

Tapper's business had suddenly grown enormously successful and Manfred, exams passed, had become indispensable. He was growing prosperous. Tapper made him a gift of the remnant of the house price and increased his salary almost two-fold. Manfred bought a car, a black Chrysler. Every weekend he drove his wife and child out of London. They day-tripped to Brighton, to Windsor, Oxford. He bought her clothes he thought she could wear with pride. He filled the house with new gewgaws. He spent heavily on his unloved son, toys and treats. The house grew thick with his purchases as he tried to keep his cooling heart warm with belongings.

By the time Martin was a year old, time had speeded up for his father. The child grew fast. It was as though the speed of his growth was stealing something precious out of

Manfred's own time. A day seemed a tiny thing; hours fell away, barely noticed. The child was taller and stronger with each week. A month would have seemed eternal for the boy but such a period was like water in the father's hands. Manfred was not yet near forty but already his son was beginning to make him feel old.

After Martin's first birthday, Emma announced her intention to return to work. Manfred was stung. It was an insult to the new prosperity he had managed to create for her. He could not bear that she might return to the department store. Such work was demeaning for her. They argued and the child cried bitterly at their noise. Manfred pointed out how little-needed her small income now was. Moreover, she was a mother and the child needed her at home at least until he began to go to school. He was surprised by the vehemence of his objections. He had not imagined that she might return to work. He had not realized how much he had come to like having her at home. He didn't know why but he knew that he could not allow her to go back to work.

In the end, she acquiesced. She gathered up the sobbing child and sat on a kitchen chair looking at her husband. It had been their bitterest argument. Her face was remote, uncharacteristic. But she acquiesced. That was all he wanted. The next day, he bought an expensive hat for her at the department store in which she had once worked. Sarah Rosen helped him choose the gift. They had never really been alone together before and she seemed uneasy. Manfred suspected a small *frisson* and was flattered. He did not tell Emma.

He was happy again now. He thought himself recovered from the shock and disequilibrium of the birth of his son. He felt that things had returned to how they were before that event. But he knew that the quality of his happiness was different. It wasn't joy. It was satisfaction. In particular, it was not happiness for Emma. He no longer felt joy in the simple fact of marriage to her. The happiness, the satisfaction was his. He was pleased with his life, wife, son and money. For the first time that he could remember, he felt that he exerted some measure of control.

He controlled his life. At work, he was necessary. Tapper had given him a job because they had been friends but now Tapper needed him. Manfred could find another job with ease. He had a wife who loved him and subdued her will to his. She was beautiful and loving. She, too, needed him. She and her child depended on him. He felt powerful but generous. Such dependence was benign if he administered it lovingly.

When the Rosens discovered that Emma was not going back to work, they had imperfectly concealed their surprise. Sarah had jokingly chided Emma on her good fortune. That would suit her admirably, she said, a husband to go out to work all day while she remained at home. But Manfred knew that she was uneasy and sympathetic. Tom had found a new job in a bank. He was better paid than Manfred, and Sarah had not begun to consider giving up her own job. Manfred was annoyed. He felt that Sarah was silently accusing him of dominating his wife.

Sarah called often. Soon she was Emma's single remaining female friend. The rest of their friends were Manfred's friends. Even Sarah, though an ex-workmate of Emma's, was the wife of one of Manfred's old school friends. The two women became closer than ever and Manfred often imagined a conspiratorial air in their friendship. He no longer liked the way Sarah looked at him. He grew jealous of her. Even Tom's habitual ease of manner had disappeared. When the two men were together, Manfred detected some discomfort in his friend, some embarrassment, evidence that he and Sarah often talked about Emma, often talked about Manfred. Manfred grew jealous of Tom too. He began to resent the tenderness with which he spoke of and to his own wife. He particularly disliked Tom making any gesture or saying any word of affection in Emma's presence. Once, Tom told a long, indulgent story about some pert remark that Sarah had made to one of her employers. He seemed comically proud of his wife's belligerence, a trait which Manfred had once admired. But as the story ended and he saw Emma blush deep, he was angry with his friend and the evening ended abruptly.

Emma was uncomplaining throughout. She was as loving and beautiful as ever. Her manner had barely changed. She was even quieter than before perhaps, and particularly when Martin was present, but she loved Manfred as much as she had ever loved him. He knew that he was doing her harm. Her silent, loving endurance told him that. The more vulnerable or weak she seemed, the greater his conviction that he was doing wrong and the greater his appetite for doing it.

But he still loved her. He would have said that he loved her more than ever. But the love had warped. Now he found it difficult to meet her eyes. She saw this and tried to reassure him, to love and obey him more. Sometimes, he tried to convince himself that he was worrying too much. When he saw her play with Martin, she seemed happier than he had ever seen her. He was guilty over nothing. *He* had given her this child she loved so much. He had given her this house *he* loved so much. But two incidents, two small moments, destroyed this comfort.

The first was a winter morning when he bumbled around the house getting ready for work. Outside the sky was still black and the prospect of leaving for work (even in his beloved car) seemed bleak and chilly. As he knotted his tie in the kitchen, he felt aggrieved. Emma would be able to stay at home in the warm (she had lit a fire already) bright house. He turned to where she was sitting at the kitchen table with Martin on her lap, preparing to make some remark about her enviable domestic prospect. She had picked up the newspaper with her free hand and was closely examining a folded page. Manfred was surprised. She never really read newspapers. He moved closer. She was reading the list of the day's radio programmes. He flushed with shame. He had diminished her to this. For the first time, he imagined the ten heavy hours that she had to pass while he was at work. Martin had only just begun to speak. She might have gone out but she would still have been alone with the child – Sarah would be at work. Her days were long and solitary. The radio must be vital to her day. Its noise would be her only comfort or intercourse. She looked up at him as he stood over her. Surprised at the sudden tenderness in his face, she put the newspaper back on the table and took his hand in hers. She asked him what was wrong.

'Nothing,' he replied.

The following spring, Manfred returned home late from work. It was his birthday and he knew that Emma had expected him hours ago. She would be disappointed. Wearily, he prepared himself for some mute reproach.

But none came. She was bright and affectionate, almost as though she were glad to see him at all. (The desperation of this affection annoyed him more than reproach.) Martin had waited up for Manfred's return since it was his father's birthday, an eminently special occasion. The child, however, had fallen asleep and lay now on a sofa with a blanket over him, his face flushed scarlet with postponed sleep. He touched the boy's hair lightly and Martin stirred querulously in his slumber. Emma wished him a happy birthday and kissed him, stepping onto her toes to reach his cheek. Manfred flinched slightly and felt foolish.

'I'll get some wine,' he said.

He found it when he was looking for a corkscrew. It was a cake. On the top lay seven square sheets of wafer into which had been cut seven letters, one on each sheet. Chocolate had been poured into the gaps and had set in the shape of those seven letters. The M at the beginning and the D at the end were larger than the other characters. The letters spelt his name. They were intricate and laborious. She had made this herself. It must have taken hours of painstaking labour. Perhaps Martin had helped. That might have been why he tried to stay up so late and wait for Manfred's return and the moment when he saw the cake. That was why Emma had hidden it in a cupboard so that she might show it to him when the boy was present.

The cake wounded him. It must have taken all day. It was an object unworthy of her time and care. For a moment he sensed the industry and desire for industry that he was trying to smother in her. This simple small thing, so worked and perfect. It should have been a laughable guilt, an over-worked husband sorry to have ruined such a careful treat, but it goaded him like pain. This was all that he was allowing her to do with her time, with her life. He pushed the cake back into the cupboard and closed the door on that tiny fact of love.

THAT night he had sneaked out of their bed without disturbing her and had crept downstairs. He had looked at the cake again and revelled in guilt. He passed the night on the armchair in his study, smoking bitter cigarettes. He felt like a small, small man and promised himself that he would change. He had been committing a silent, husband's crime. Martin was nearly three years old. There was no reason that she should not go back to work. They could find a nursery or somesuch. Her life was hers to measure and order. He could not rob her of that. The cake had done it all. Things would change. He would not try to trim her to fit his shape. He would give her back her world.

But the next day, he was small again. A week later he

had shrunk further still and after a month had passed he had dwindled so much that the cake was a memory of shame, an unbidden, unwelcome rush of blood to his face. By the time his next birthday had come round, he had forgotten the cake almost entirely. And he was less than a small man.

NINE

DAWN. London was rufous and deplorable. The sun rubbed the streets into the warmthless tinge of shaving rash and Manfred's thoughts turned to all the headaches he had ever had. Dawn. The street was bedraggled and lugubrious. London seemed sorry but without good excuse.

Manfred's spirits slumped in the typical meagreness of this London dawn. After such a bad night, he had looked to first light with sleepless optimism. He had hoped that it would ease that pain, that it would forgive that sin. But day didn't wash those stains. For the all-night sufferer, dawn is always a disappointment. This dawn was typical.

Across the street, Manfred noticed a familiar figure. It was the young whore he had dealt with after Webb's argument of the other morning. The girl who had returned his money. She must have been one of the regulars on this strip. She obviously now considered her night's business done with and had donned a pair of spectacles. Manfred smiled sadly at this small inaptitude. It changed the girl's entire figure. The spectacles lent her an air of weakness. He was annoyed to feel a definite launch of sexual interest. She should have tried wearing them while she worked. Patently, some men might like a whore who wore glasses. As well as improving her general vision. But perhaps that was just it – why she didn't wear them. Perhaps the local haze of the purblind made her work easier.

Manfred considered hailing her. It might be misunderstood. She looked the height of happiness standing there alone, heels and hair, while her beaux, a million spent men, dreamed away the last of their sleep. Indeed, she seemed now to be weeping. Her shoulders were hunched and her head drooped. Was she lighting a cigarette? No. Manfred spied a renegade glint of misery from under her glasses. The old man was almost cheered. It seemed such a sensible response to the prevailing facts. She must have done a lot of crying behind those glasses.

Manfred moved on, ashamed. Again the girl made him think of Emma. Emma had cried a lot without the aid of glasses. He was comfortable now that whores reminded him of his wife. He had worked it all out. It was merely that most women a man met were something else as well. Something besides women. They had jobs, families, names, opinions and objections. They were people, demonstrably complex. Men thought whores were women in emphasis (or an idea of women in emphasis). That was how they earned their wage. They were paid for the accident of their gender.

A truck passed slowly, dripping some obscure soupiness as it went. A derelict pigeon strutted across to inspect. It took a speculative peck before deciding to breakfast elsewhere. The full day was establishing itself quickly now. The light was thickening, beginning to etch slanted beams and shadows, routing the vague pink seepage of a few minutes previous.

Manfred's step accelerated as his vexatious belly responded to the nugatory glory of the morning. His scrupulous pigeon began to emit a series of pellets in a tight radius of its twitching tail feathers. It yodelled softly and Manfred envied the creature its easy toilet. He was growing tired of London. Too many moods were suitable to this city, too many despairs found their home here. Years ago, his claims of London birth had made him feel a more substantial man, an heir to its exquisitely European close-up grime. But now ordure was setting in, animal, vegetable and mineral.

A young man wearing a grey hood crossed the deserted

street in front of him carrying a television set. His gait was blithe and unimpeachable. He noticed Manfred and stopped to wait as the old man approached him.

'Wanna buy a television?' he asked.

Manfred smiled neutrally and declined the offer. He wished he had seemed firmer. Gentiles often mistook politeness for weakness. The young man seemed undaunted. Manfred had now stopped rather than risk trouble by walking past.

'You can have it for twenty quid.'

'No, really, thank you.'

'Fifteen.'

'Thank you, no.'

'Gimme a tenner and you can have it.'

'I don't have any money.' Manfred's unease increased. The youth's eyes were horribly bloodshot, stained by some nameless excess. His mouth now quivered with annoyance.

'Come on, for fuck's sake. Gimme a fiver. Five quid for a telly. That's a fucking steal.' His voice was thick and sluggish. A tiny overture of raindrops spattered his hood. He repeated his offer. 'Go on. A fiver.'

Manfred wondered how stupid or dangerous this boy might be. He had no choice.

'I'm sorry but I have no money.'

'Fuck it.' The boy tried to smile but his mouth trembled too much to achieve the effect. The rain was growing steady. Under his hood, the young man now seemed fragile and desperate. The dreadful quiver of his lips increased.

'Ah, you can have it anyway.'

He stepped back from Manfred and heaved the television into the air above his head. He skipped back as the set crashed to the ground at the old man's feet, splintering and smashing with a weary thud. His uncontrollable features registered pleasure as he looked at the wounded television.

He tried to smile his jerky smile at Manfred. 'You could have had that for a fiver, you old wanker.'

He walked away in the direction from which he had come. His grey hood was already darkening with rain and his retreating figure was drab and sad in the drizzle. Manfred stood over the crippled television set like a mourner at a graveside. He pulled his overcoat closer round him. That archaic garment afforded him little protection against the desultory rain. His neck was growing wet.

The old man waited until the young man was out of sight before moving on. He tried to dismiss him from his thoughts. The boy's incendiary face had scared him, more for the boy than for himself. Walking the streets at earliest dawn with his strange burden, the youth had seemed like an apparition – boisterously unlikely. And despite his warlike spasm he had seemed frail and restless, feeble prey to the rain and the wind's cold dismissal.

Manfred walked past the housing estate into which the youth had disappeared. The rain, though gentle, was already spotting and staining its greys. The old man was pressed by an abrupt desire to return home. His room seemed a jealous refuge from the drained streets, the myopic prostitute, her city-centre circumstances and now this half-crazed youth. Sometimes in his new senescence the city was too crowded, too many moulds and shapes, too many people, too many lights and darks, too much damned chiaroscuro.

The regular falsetto hum of a milk float glided by. Already cleaners were standing at their bus stops, colourful and redoubtable in the grime. He passed a group of bench-seated matrons whose legs bulged out from under their skirts like a row of fleshy vases. Their conversation was vivid and formless, making him hungry for their firm vitality. He envied them their industry and incontinent zest. He recalled other dawn walks punctuated by such women. Many of his successes and happinesses had been celebrated by a dawn walk, after nights when he had been too happy or too proud to sleep.

He had walked the dawn on the day after his wedding. Emma had slept, after all. He had watched her three or four hours, his stomach fermenting with love. He had never watched someone sleep before and as the hours passed, he grew overwhelmed with tenderness. His love grew too big for the small room and he felt himself suffocating under its weight. He had dressed quietly and stolen out into the streets in the moist first light. As he walked, he lit many cigarettes and thought of her. His love grew yet, stretching out in street and sky. He watched the early workers and late stragglers and fancied that they knew him, that they were kindled by the enormity of his love, as though, rampant in him, it had planted seeds in all their fortunate hearts. London filled as he built a city of love. Untricked by memory, it didn't seem like yesterday. It seemed more painful years distant. It seemed like the dead grief for a dead dream.

The memory had halted him and he stood now, irresolute and ragged with pain. The rain persisted and his body felt suddenly heavy with sleeplessness. An ambulance clattered and yelled towards and beyond him. He looked at its black windows and did not wonder what grief went there. He passed his hand across his face to wipe away some raindrops. His face felt pitted and drab. His face had ebbed and fallen with age. It had shrunk on his skull. Only his nose had grown.

> *The Lord said unto Moses*
> *All Jews shall have big noses*
> *All excepting Aaron*
> *For he shall have a square 'un.*

Abruptly he decided to turn back and walk home. He was tired now, sleepy. He passed a shop window filled with televisions which had been switched on through the night.

The screens were all filled with faint pebbledash motion. Nothing was being broadcast. Without pictures, the machines seemed thwarted and foolish. The flurry of tiny dots seemed to express their impotence and fury. He moved on, feeling unreasonably victorious.

The cleaning women were still waiting at their bus stop. Neither the steady rain nor the waiting had deterred their fervent chatter.

'She didn't, did she?'

'I'm telling you.'

'Did you hear that, Sue?'

'I'm not a bit surprised.'

'Did I hear what?'

'Surely not.'

'Oh, yes.'

'What? Did I hear what?'

A passing van with an open window left a half-heard snatch of radio music in its wake. High above, a slit between the clouds allowed a brief moment of brilliance to warm the damp street. Almost in answer, the rain fell marginally harder.

To quell the thoughts of Emma that the sudden memory had brought, Manfred inspected the posters on the walls and windows of the streets. A travel agent's vistas and views yielded no comfort. Their blue was too blue, their beauty, though beauty still, was too bland. A huge hoarding across the street was better. It lauded a new motor car surrounded by a clutch of impossibly beautiful half-naked women. Its urgent klaxon of greed and venery stunned him sufficiently and his mind was comfortably numbed.

His mind was so successfully numbed that he failed to notice the wrecked television over which he tripped and fell. His right hand and forearm took the brunt of the fall. Momentarily stupid with shock, he believed that he had been struck and he rolled onto his back to see his non-existent attacker. His left elbow poked into the shattered remnants of the television screen and he briefly struggled to free his coat from its metal innards. He inspected his right hand and saw blood and grit on fingers and palm. Some of the flesh had laddered like tights and a small flap had opened over his wrist bone, cufflike.

The first presages of pain lit up as he palpated the flesh on his forearm. He knew that he had broken no bones and was surprised at the quality of the pain in his hand and arm. It seemed truly inordinate. Inevitably, his other pain took the opportunity to reappear, afflicting his gut with punctilious severity. He shifted into a more comfortable position and rested his head against the television set as his belly blew its gale. From the pavement he watched dispassionately as a busful of astonished faces trundled past towards the women he had just passed. For one terrible moment as the thorn in his flesh moved deeper in him, he thought he had soiled himself. He prayed that the cleaning women would board their bus without coming to his aid. He hoped that they might think he was drunk and thus a waste of their jaded charity. He waited, shamed and terrified, until he heard their bus move off again.

His torso flared into a new series of galling cramps. Stricken, maddened, the old man tried to raise himself but fell back against the broken television. In lunatic inspiration, he grabbed his injured right hand and squeezed the wounds hard. The shock almost caused him to faint but the mortification of his hand effectively deadened the riot in his belly. Cradling his livid arm, he moaned softly to himself. His eyes filled with cloudy tears and he wretchedly noted the success of this new analgesic technique.

For a few minutes Manfred lay still on the wet pavement. The rain fell yet but the old man was content to remain inert. His flesh seemed bled of sensation. From where he lay he mutely inspected a small clump of grass and weeds at the foot of a lamp-post. Unorthodox garbage was sown in the midst of the little vegetation. A workman's coarse glove, fingers puffed and full-looking. One half of a pair of cheap sunglasses. A beer can painted gold and heavily lettered in rococo gilt yet still irredeemably sordid. Several wisps of soaked newsprint. A box of dead matches.

Manfred's reverie was disrupted as he heard footsteps. He looked up and saw Webb's whore walking towards him. She had obviously clocked off and decided to go home. Manfred was horrified. He tried to raise himself from the pavement but fell back. Though the pain had largely subsided, his body seemed moribund and unmanageable. He coloured with shame as the girl approached. This insolent female seemed to bedevil his every recent step. He was conscious of the absurdity of his lying on the pavement in the rain among the ruins of a stolen television. She would tell Webb and that lunatic barbarian would have more details to fuel his gross humours. His ears ached with clamour and his arms pulsed with extra blood. Despite his humiliation, he prepared a face with which to meet the girl's enquiries or laughter.

But her approach was hesitant, her step alternately rapid and broken. Though she had obviously recognized Manfred, she seemed to be searching for a way of stepping around or over his prostrate form without having to acknowledge him. Since the old man effectively blocked the inside of the pavement, the girl was forced to walk around him near the kerb. As she passed him, she raised her hand to cover the left side of her face. Manfred watched her, amazed. Her foot kicked the golden beer can spinning into the road and she fled by.

Manfred lay back again. Her shielding hand had not covered the grievous contusion that fouled her face. He had easily seen her inflamed eye, her stricken jaw and the molten swelling all along the left side of her face. Thus the glasses, thus the tears. It was that story. It was that old story.

Whatever blow it had been, whatever arm, it had marked her well.

Carefully, with infinite, tender precision, the old man gained his feet and stood steady for a full two minutes before moving on slowly.

THE first time Manfred hit Emma it had seemed like a tentative experiment not to be repeated. Like a man firing a gun to see what it felt like or a child touching candle-flame to tutor himself against doing it again. He could not now remember many of the details or any of the preceding argument. He was left with a single clear memory of Emma opening the bedroom door in the middle of the night and himself arresting her progress. He had pulled her back, his hand strong and rough on her arm. She stared at him for a moment, her hair disordered and her face flushed, and then he struck her firmly across the face with his open hand. Her head had jerked back from the force of the blow and her hair hid her face completely. He relaxed his grip on her arm and they had stood there for some minutes. Emma's head hung low in front of him, curtained by her hair. Without looking at him, she had retraced her steps and climbed back into their bed. When Manfred joined her, she turned away from him leaving her hand resting on his hip as a consolation. Though conscious that she was silently awake, Manfred soon fell asleep.

The next day he felt much remorse. However, he also felt strangely elated. Indeed, in one sense it had been a success. He had at last done the thing he had always feared. He had struck her. He had done the worst that he could do and knew now that he could never do such a thing again. He was almost proud that he had rid himself of that violence in such a small way. One blow was a meagre price to pay for the ending of any possibility of other violence. As he sat listening to Tapper's usual acquisitive rambling, he even felt that he had done himself more harm than he had done to her. The strong vivid shame he felt was more than any pain he could have caused her. This lapse had cleaned him of violence. Last night's blow had set him free.

THE second time Manfred hit Emma it felt like the start of something. It was a testing of the water for him and for her. They knew then that there was much more to inflict and endure. A new secret opened between them.

It had happened quickly, with almost seamless ease. They went out to dinner with the Rosens in a restaurant near the nightclub they had all frequented years before. Such treats had become rare. A neighbour's daughter was taking care of Martin for the evening and Manfred was tense with the unaccustomed festivity. Emma's mood was sparkling and vivacious. She and Sarah bantered across the table and Manfred was shamed by how long it had been since he had seen his wife so happy.

Then Sarah began to tell them about a book she was reading. It was a holocaust book. She talked about it at length and Emma grew visibly uneasy. Manfred was surprised at Sarah. She knew Emma's history well enough. Tom, too, seemed embarrassed quickly, as though he and Sarah had discussed this already. Perhaps the foolish woman thought that this might be a way to draw Emma out, make her talk about the things she kept secret. In the midst of a gloating description of Nazi rape, Manfred looked mutely at his wife and saw an uncontrollable, terrible blush spread across her face. He felt sick. She had never been able to control her blushes. They constantly betrayed her. And now, at Sarah's rape story, she blushed more than he had ever seen her blush.

The rest of the evening was blind. A blur of noise and faces. He was filled with rage. This new suspicion choked him. By the time they had parted from the Rosens, he was cold with fury. When they got home, he remained downstairs, mad with hatred, while she went upstairs and prepared for bed. He smoked a fevered cigarette and then followed her upstairs.

The first punch (and perhaps that was the moment, throwing a closed hand at her, perhaps that was what broke all the rules), the first punch had been thrown blind. His arm had flushed with blood, independent blood that gave him strength and strange blamelessness. It landed on the side of her head and they had both reeled with the shock. From that moment he began to feel such shame, such terrible hatred for himself. The only step was to hit her more and hit her harder – to lose his shame and rage in destroying her. He punched her again – head, shoulders, body – the blows less accurate as she desperately tried to scramble away from his fury. Soon, the beating began to take on a curious logic. There was a certain amount of harm he had to do. Until that was completed, he did not have to think about other options. The pain in his fists became his guide to his progress as she crashed against the wall, the door, the floor. The weight of his blows did not, could not, subside. He felt matchlessly strong and confident. Euphoric with power and rectitude.

After a few moments, she broke under his blows and could only try to save herself as best she could. She tried to crawl under the bed. Like an ape, he crouched over and brought his fists down massively on her flanks.

It finished quite abruptly. He stopped to draw breath. His rage dissolved, making him feel limp and weary. For some moments he squatted over her, panting rapidly. He was dispassionate, even puzzled. He looked down at his wife. He saw blood on her nightdress. Her hair covered her face. Her legs were bruising already. Her torso seemed oddly misshapen, like beaten dough. His fists began to throb with their own pain. He wondered what to do.

At work the next day, Manfred carried out his tasks with heedless efficiency. Tapper was away and he could see out the day without much concentration. Inwardly, he retraced the beating again and again. The day was warm and he sweated with dread. He had removed his jacket and rolled up his shirt sleeves. His hands and forearms were darkly bruised and even swollen here and there where the blows had been particularly dreadful. His right elbow was mushy and sore from when he had elbowed her in the face, a blow he knew had damaged her perhaps most of all. It's not the heavy hand that counts, it's the sharp elbow that wins the day. He knew what this had done, what it could not have failed to do to Emma's flesh. He had crawled out of the house early that morning without disturbing her. He could not imagine what she might now look like, what integral harm he might have done her.

All morning his mouth was dry, swollen and rough. No amount of tea or glasses of water moistened his tongue. His throat was unquenchable, hot and chafing. He laboured under the constant suspicion that everyone knew what he had done. The office girls looked at him differently, with what he suspected was the special kind of contempt reserved for wife-beaters. He dreaded the thought that the Rosens might call on Emma. The thought that she might be visited became obsessive and terrifying. He resolved to sneak home at lunch-time.

His hands shook so much he could not trust himself to drive. He took a taxi and sweated further on the leather seat. He could barely croak the destination to the cab driver. He paused outside his house and looked sadly at that precious property. It suddenly seemed no comfort at all, no foundation on which to build. His home had changed already – some tiny but significant disorder had occurred. He felt bricked-up with despair. He felt quite unmanned.

He opened the front door softly and crept indoors. Inside, it was worse. His home accused him. Each small domestic object reproached him. Their comfort, their very familiarity seemed lost to him now. The long white umbrella stand, the chubby telephone on its table, the mute row of Emma's coats and the lower row of hooks from which his son's hung.

The house was silent. There was no clue to where Emma might be. None the less, Manfred started to climb the stairs with some unknown certainty, creeping like a thief through his own house. The staircase seemed endless and obdurate. His pace slowed as he climbed.

He paused outside their bedroom door. Though the silence in the house was as complete and pervasive as ever, he was conscious that his wife was in the bedroom. The door was ajar. He crouched and pushed it gently, widening the crack between door and wall.

Emma stood naked near the foot of the bed, slightly turned from him. Her dress lay in a formless puddle at her feet. She was looking at herself in the full length mirror on the wardrobe. Manfred could not see her reflection but her flank and much of her spine was visible to him. Her flesh was disfigured in many places. Her back was richly sown with bruises and scratches as though his hand had dabbed and smeared those marks upon her. Her flesh, rib, hip and haunch, was roused and wounded.

A great black bruise lay on her hip, plate sized, and her legs were spotted with bruises and cuts, large and small. Her hair hid her face and this somehow made it worse. There was more horror in the evidence of his hatred on her faceless, blameless flesh. His throbbing hands felt remote, alien. He clasped them uselessly. It was their fault, those bad hands.

Still, she had not moved. The fixity with which she stared at her naked self frightened him. It was as though she was fastening the image of her damaged body in her memory. Sealing this testimony against him. He wished that she would move and dispel this grim inertia. He sensed that he could not move until she did. But she remained motionless, staring at the mirror, her face hidden in her wheat-coloured hair, naked and broken.

Then she turned. Her breasts and belly were crushed and discoloured. One nipple had flared purple and inflamed. Her shoulders were uniformly blackened, dead blood under the skin. His wife's eyes met his without reproach.

THE rain had finished and the clouds were lifting slowly in the sky. Pallid sunlight laboured over the rooftops. Manfred felt that his heart was glass and broken. His face was hot with grief. The height of the sky seemed appropriate. When happy, his skies had always been high. April, May and June. This was a dolorous morning – low-ceilinged, misery-making.

He was nearly home now. The streets were filling with their second complement. The cleaning women had moved on now and their place was taken by newsagents opening up their shops, postmen, vanfuls of workmen. The wet streets shone like steel – indeed, in the pallor and damp, much of the world seemed metal. Inland gulls flew low, shrieking and greedy.

He crossed the street towards his flat. He saw that the window above his was bright with soft light. Garth was awake, whether he was preparing for or just returning from work was hard to say. The boy seemed to work long and varied hours. Needless to say, Webb's curtains were drawn. Webb never rose early. He struggled to rise at all and when he did he seldom dressed before three or four o'clock in the afternoon. Latterly, he had been in the habit of paying Manfred lunchtime calls; sitting at the table in varieties of *déshabillé*.

A ginger cat sat on the mat on the doorstep. Its fur was ragged and spiky with rain. As Manfred bent to stroke its back, the cat arched and growled amiably. The creature looked miserable and weary. The old man opened the front door. If the cat would come in with him, he would give it some breakfast. He clucked and chirruped invitingly at the animal and moved inside. He held the door open and beckoned the cat once more. The cat stood watching him for a moment. Its front paws quivered slightly as though it would enter but in the end it turned away and trotted, high-tailed, down the steps into the garden. Manfred closed the door sadly.

As he passed the door to Webb's flat he heard the sound of two people snoring. It seemed Webb preferred that his women should stay the night these days. He thought of Webb's other girl, the one he had seen that morning. It seemed unjust. Her smashed, stricken face would have meant little to Webb. Her temporary disfigurement was no hindrance to him. London had lots of whores.

He opened his own door. For a man who had never slept with a prostitute, he seemed to have encountered an excessive number of them. Practically the only women he had seen during the war had been whores – Egypt, Libya and Italy. Berlin in '46 and '47 had swarmed with tarts. Thousands of women and girls patrolled the streets of the broken city, rolling their skirts up among the rubble for a dollar or a jar of coffee. Thin girls and fat girls, old girls and young girls whose breasts had not yet grown. The occupying armies had sullied the city and the prevalence of whores meant that all women suffered the coarseness of the soldiers. Women turned whore in desperation, war wrought a terrible change in what they felt precious. The men, the soldiers, stayed the same but revelled in the licence of damaged Berlin. Once Manfred stumbled upon a twelve-year-old girl fellating a massive Ulsterman from the Pay Corps. The Irish corporal had buttoned himself up hurriedly but the girl had remained kneeling in front of him. A sergeant by now, Manfred had put the corporal on a charge but he could do nothing about the girl. He knew that he had merely robbed her of a fee and that she would be kneeling in front of some other soldier within the hour.

The women of Berlin were beaten and even murdered regularly. Mutilated bodies were discovered all over the city, naked, broken and displayed like a bag of rejected sweets. Even the Berliners turned against their women and killed or wounded them. As though the German men, humiliated by the great failure of their arms, had used up the remnants of their hatred and their militarism upon their women.

In the bathroom Manfred filled the washbasin with tepid water and began to clean the wound on his hand. The water soothed and tiny clots of dark blood broke off from his skin and dissolved into pink eddies and swirls. Outside the frosted bathroom window, the morning had become almost lavish. He opened the window with his uninjured left hand. Profuse light filled the room and the bloody water in the basin glittered like bright wine.

PART THREE

MANFRED'S PAIN

TEN
(1959–62)

THEIR marriage crumbled. It had been the house that Manfred built and now its masonry had rotted like a carious tooth. The first time he hit her, he was sure that it hurt him more than her. Hers had been a mote of pain compared with the energy and extent of his own guilt and remorse. The second time he beat her, he was polluted with shame. A pattern had been cut and copied. More such work would come. Revulsion, fear and a whole range of mortifications punished him. Thinking always of himself, he grieved at a substantial discount.

His home became a reproach to him. The objects with which they had crammed the house seemed an old dream of stability and permanence. Now, the very building seemed to mock the substance of his marriage, his manhood and self. He no longer lingered on the doorstep with his hand on the bricks by the door. Real estate had lost its remote domestic solace.

Emma began to lurk in the house. She sought the deepest shadows and lit the lamps later and later. Then they would sit silently in the widening gloom with their noiseless son, just as Manfred had sat with his mother and brothers twenty-five years before. She started taking the boy out at the weekend. Circuses, zoos and parks. Though she did not openly avoid her husband, Martin knew that something was wrong and began to regard his father with childish suspicion and dread.

The third time Manfred hit Emma, it was getting easy. It was as though he had lost his violence virginity. After a couple of attempts, it could be seemly and free of true remorse. The fourth time he beat her, he cried and begged forgiveness. They tumbled into tearful sex on the ruined bed. Afterwards, she held him tight, her hair damp and wild as a hothouse shrub. He nearly told himself she liked it. The fifth time he beat her, he lost count.

Now all he did seemed marred and bloodied by that violence. When he was at the office, his mind wandered. His face would flush abruptly and nausea would bubble suddenly in his throat. His inattention ruined his work. Tapper complained, but lazily. He was preoccupied with a series of enigmatic deals with men who didn't give their name over the telephone. Manfred's own preoccupation went largely unnoticed. From eight thirty to five o'clock, he sweated out the day, dreading the return to his silent, accusing home. His working hours were sawdust to him.

Meals were silent and tortuous. Martin hated dining with his father. The boy would sit rigid with tension, his drawn face imperfectly chewing his tasteless food. Sometimes he was so tense that he would lurch from the table and his parents would listen to the distant sounds of their son vomiting and crying in the bathroom. Manfred began to fear the boy as his own father had feared him. Martin looked at him with the unassailable rectitude of childhood.

His nights, too, were tortured. He no longer lay awake and watched her while she slept. He knew that it was now she who lay awake and vigilant, fearing some new blow. He fell asleep with ease but his sleep became unmanageable, exhausting. He dreamed that he battered Emma in the kitchen. He threw plates at her that would not break. In his fury, his arms sawed through the air. She broke apart in his hands, her bones splitting and cracking as though he was clearing a path through tall grass. She lay on the floor, cracked open among the unbroken plates. Like a horse, her bones would not knit. He had destroyed her. He would wake remorsefully, his arms cradling her while she pretended to sleep.

He started drinking. He experimented with a number of options. Whisky, brandy, vodka and rum. They all made him sick. He chose gin. It too made him sick but less catastrophically so. He drank in bars, at work. He drank when he came home. He stayed out and stayed in, drinking as much as he could soak. He developed a taste for the most squalid bars and would often end up sweating in the toilets, his hot face resting on slimy tiles, his nostrils choked with the smell of his own gin-bright piss.

When he was drunk, he naturally beat her more and harder. He would stumble home dull with anger, drooling and gross. Her very placidness angered and accused him. Still reeking with the filth of some poky bar, he would confront and harm her. If he stayed at home and drank, the hours before bed would pass so slowly and his wife and son would move through their house so softly that his rage would stoke itself inexorably. By the time Martin was put to bed (and soon the child delayed that as long as possible – seeing his presence as some protection for his mother), the hatred would ignite. His now-proficient hands would move against her.

Certain bruises, certain marks on her became constant, as though they were his favourite target. A belt of marks always lay across her shoulders and down her arms like black sunburn. An open hand did unexpected damage. The marks on her were difficult to hide and when he happened to notice them, he would be sick with anger.

But when he hit her, he loved her much more. When he hit her he thought of her more. He cherished her more. He needed her more. The beatings were unselfish. They were ardent. He ached for his hurt wife. He had used to dream her dead and admire that passion of his grief and loss. Now he damaged her and pitied her with a choking, guilty tenderness. He exulted in the extent and luxury of his pity. He beat her, he pitied her, he loved her more.

They never spoke of the harm that he did and she suffered. After the earliest incidents, a protocol of silence was established. It seemed to be a shame they both bore. The late evenings, after their son had gone to bed, were tense with unspoken sorrow. He was amazed that she never reprimanded him. There must have been much she wanted to say, deny or protest. She never did. Sometimes, she looked at him with some particular gravity or stillness. There were moments when her face held all her vulnerability and strength but she never protested. Perhaps she waited for some revolt in him, some halt that never came.

Somehow, it had all gone wrong. He realized how wrong that was when one day he moved to embrace her in a sudden access of affection. She stood by the stove in the kitchen, warm light filtered around her. As his arms stretched to touch her, she flinched from him. He stood useless, his arms empty and his heart full and sick as she cowered before him. As usual, she said nothing but her bent figure, her victim's face were all he needed to know. For the rest of that day anger and shame filled him. That night he beat her out of shame, out of fear.

The violence increased with a mordant logic. It wasn't that something in him had died. Something in him had been born and grown strong and wicked. He was surprised at what he could now do. It seemed he could harm her with pellucid ease. Each blow against her was another self-pollution. When he was alone, he seethed with formless rancour. Outside his home, he grew suspicious and defensive. Other men, colleagues and strangers, held a special reproof. Their manhood seemed replete and healthy. He felt himself to be a loathsome thing – woman-beater, coward. He watched men in the street. He felt the contempt they would have felt if they had known his secret. He speculated about individual men, chosen for their raincoats, stature or haircuts. He knew that they would never have beaten Emma. He burned with lunatic jealousy.

Emma suffered more for these jealousies. He was terrified that she might betray him; that she might tell some upright man of her suffering. He began to watch her like a spy. He hated to see her silent, not to know what she was thinking, what betrayal lay there. He knew that she spent hours staring at mirrors, still and silent. Once he stood at the open door and restlessly waited for her to notice his presence. Her expression was clandestine and sad. Her eyes were steady, her lips closed softly but firmly.

Every day, now, he would catch her staring at herself in a mirror, gravely and minutely inspecting her face. Her stillness and concentration unnerved him. He wondered what she saw in the glass. What evidence of harm. He grew jealous of the mirrors as well. For a time he considered hiding or destroying them. His courage failed him, however, and they remained where they hung or stood throughout the house. He suspected that she was inspecting the harm he had done her or perhaps the harm that others had done her, the wartime, Jewish harm about which she never spoke.

He was now jealous of that as well. In truth, he had always been jealous of Emma's nameless wartime past. He was jealous of other things. He was jealous of the bus in which she had ridden to school. He was jealous of the skirts and shoes she had worn, of the sounds she'd heard, sights she'd seen and thoughts she'd thought. In the face of her unimpeachable sexual fidelity, he could only be jealous of everything. He was jealous of her house and her son. But most of all, he was jealous of the war, of the camps. He had beaten her first because of a suspicion of some childhood violation or rape at Birkenau. He was jealous of Birkenau.

They no longer saw their friends. The Rosens had protested for a few months but eventually they left Manfred and his family alone, correctly suspecting some difficulty in the marriage. The very last of Emma's old work-friends also fell away. After a few weeks of Manfred answering the door to these women, they knew the trouble and stayed away. He forbade the trips that Emma and Martin had been taking to avoid him, even to the old aunt. The house was a gaol. Now all three skulked around the rooms in lonely patterns. The boy became mutely seditious. Manfred knew that when his back was turned his son vented his little rage by contorting his face and making violent gestures at his father. This thwarted mime of hatred wounded the man. He realized now that he could nurture no dreams of repair. His son hated him, his son wanted him dead or gone.

Then, quite abruptly, Emma stopped speaking altogether. Manfred had arrived home one night in August when the sky was full of moon and cloud. He had been drinking in a bar near King's Cross. The bar had been too loathsome even for him and he had left earlier than he initially intended. He let himself in quietly (as he always did now) and climbed the stairs. Emma came to the top of the staircase hurriedly. She had heard him arrive. He knew that she had been watching herself in the mirror. Dull anger swept him (as it always did now). He turned away and went into the kitchen. His son was there, sitting at the table reading a book. He did not look up as Manfred took off his coat and hat. Emma followed him into the kitchen and Manfred gave her a surly greeting. She smiled timidly and moved towards the stove. He would have been angry if she had not looked so frightened (as she always did now).

He only realized what was happening when they were half-way through their meal. The boy had been sedulously talkative and in his surprise at this, Manfred had barely noticed that his wife had not spoken. While they ate, however, the boy's volubility faltered and a reek of silence descended. After a few minutes, the incidental impacts of cutlery and plate had grown cacophonic and unbearable. Hesitantly, Manfred offered some neutral comment about the meal. No one answered him. He swallowed his next mouthful with difficulty and tried again, this time commenting mildly on the beauty of the evening. Again, there was silence. He was scared now. Emma's head was lowered, her hair concealing her face but Martin was staring at him with clear-eyed loathing. Manfred's throat was drying and the food was cess in his gut. He thought that he would choke. Finally, he dragged his eyes from his son's glare and turning to his wife, he asked her a direct question. She did not reply. He repeated himself.

'How was your day?'

It felt foolish and useless in his mouth. It was no challenge to the silence upon which she had decided. He waited. She did not answer.

He did not beat her that night. Defeated, he lay beside her as she pretended to sleep. Fear lay on him like a counterpane and he felt sluggish and small. He could feel the frugal heat from her body warm the bed and he tried to inch away from that strong warmth. In the dark precincts of the bed, she seemed massive. Her silence had been maintained for the whole night. There had been no obvious provocation in it. Her face had not been defiant. If anything she had seemed more meek than usual. That was the terrible detail. He might have crushed a defiant silence but a victim silence he could not subdue.

When he returned home from work the next day, the silence continued. Again he did not beat her. This unspoken truce continued for the next few days. But dreadful and frightening as her silence was, Manfred knew that the violence had not ended. He hoped that she did not imagine that.

After a week, her silence lost its horror for him. He knew then that he would hurt her again and hurt her more. The day before her thirtieth birthday he left work early and went to a cheap bar near his home. He drank without pleasure. The surly barman snubbed him and the other drinkers favoured him with contemptuous looks. The night began to feel final. Within a few hours, the entire bar seemed inebriated. Only he remained sober. He drank faster and watched the sordid oblivion of the other men and women. There was a fight. A man with a bloody face stumbled out and a woman sobbed drunkenly. The place was unendurable but he waited until he was sure that his son would have been put to bed. Then he left the bar.

Outside, it had rained and the streets were wet and explicit. Scant light dripped from lights and windows. A criminal wind chilled him through his thin coat and he hurried his step. There were few people and the sound of footsteps seemed unnaturally loud and urgent. The noise angered and scared him. They sounded like the obvious steps of the uxoricide, the killer.

By the time he was home he was drunk with a slow patient anger. All night, his rage at her silence had grown while he watched the dealings of the sordid bar. Now, he searched the house for her. Downstairs, the lights were out and the rooms were quiet. She was either in the bedroom or the bathroom. Either way, he knew she would be mirror-watching. He climbed the stairs.

She was in their bedroom. She sat on the edge of the bed, staring at the mirror in front of her. Manfred stood dully in the doorway. He could see that her face was smeared and dewy with old tears. She seemed to be unconscious of his presence. She lifted her hand to her face and gently touched her wet cheek. The gesture, so tender and penitent, wounded him. He went into the bedroom.

The beating was silent apart from the dull thuds of flesh on flesh and bone on bone. Soon, spots and smears of her blood covered the carpet and the counterpane. He knew that it was the last time. The last of all times. Nothing more than this could be done. Nothing more than this could happen. In his panic he hit her harder.

When it was over, he straightened breathlessly and looked down at her.

'Why won't you talk to me?' he said.

Then she *did* talk. She washed the blood from her face and figure and changed her spattered nightdress. She limped and stumbled brokenly, talking all the while. Her voice was strange, as though she had sand in her mouth and her lips were slashed and swollen. Her face had warped and her jaw seemed buckled but she talked. The hours passed like separate hangovers and the room seemed foggy with grief and tears. She talked. He had counted out ten years waiting to hear her talk. And now something in her had ruptured and she talked without end. She talked more then than he could listen.

SHE had been called Rosza. Her mother was a soft, tall woman who wore dresses that crinkled like wrapping paper. Her father's face was hairy and dark. He wore small spectacles which he had told her were there to prevent his nose from falling off. At school, Steya Fried laughed at this and Rosza wondered why her father had lied.

She had two sisters, one tall, one short; one wicked, one good. Dana was tall and Rachel was good. Dana scolded Rosza and Rachel soothed her tears. Rosza loved Dana more. She was beautiful and imperious. Rachel's soft heart won no love.

They lived in Prague. At school, Rosza was told that Prague was the premier city of Europe. Prague was a diamond set in the brow of the world. Certainly, Rosza loved its wide stone streets and all its lights and colours. The people were like her parents. Their clothes were soft and fragrant, their faces full and grave. Even the shabby men and poor women whom she sometimes saw seemed correct and proper.

Her father was a doctor. She knew he was famous. When other adults came to visit in the tall house in which they lived, they were courteous and admiring. Sometimes, young men blushed when they shook her father's hand. She was proud then and longed to embrace him. She was his favoured child and on certain nights she would be allowed to fall asleep on the easy chair in his study while he worked late at his desk. As her eyes grew heavy, she would watch him at work, his mouth moving as he read silently to himself, his dark head bent over his papers in the pool of light from the lamp on his desk.

On her seventh birthday, her father and mother listened to the radio and wept. Rosza was wounded. She choked on tears and rage and ran to her bedroom, sobbing. Rachel followed and lay down beside her, stroking her hair and singing softly to herself. Dana was exultant. A big war had started. It was much more important than Rosza's stupid birthday. Their papa would have to fight the British and the Germans. And perhaps even the terrible Russians. No one cared about stupid Rosza.

Rosza was grief-stricken. On *her* birthday, Dana had been taken to a French circus with clowns and horses and famous Spanish acrobats. Rosza lay on her bed and cried so much she made herself ill. When her father came, she was silent and bitter. She turned her hot face away from his hand. But he spoke gently to her and gave her medicine to drink. She cried softer now. She cried with pity to see herself so small and sad. She fell asleep with her hand wound tight around her father's unbuttoned shirt sleeve and when she woke she found that he was still sitting there, though it was now dark. He was watching her and his face was sad. In the gloom his white shirt sleeves glowed faintly against his black waistcoat and she loved him very much. In a voice trembling with sleepiness, she asked him if he was going to be a soldier and die. He promised her that he would not die and told her that the war would soon be over. The bad men would lose. Remember, he said with a smile, in the end the wicked will always grow weak while the good prosper.

But all the adults, all the men and women whom her father and mother knew seemed to disagree. The big thing that had happened in the Sudetenland had now happened to the whole of Czechoslovakia. Men asked whether the foreign armies would be firm, loyal, brave. Her father's hospital was sandbagged and a gun battery appeared on its roof one day. No one was surprised but Rosza. Rachel was frightened and Dana was gleeful and excited. But the adult world seemed to find no newness in the thing they all feared.

When she first saw all the new soldiers, she was not frightened. They were beautiful and strong. The Czech men and women feared or hated these new soldiers but to Rosza they seemed brighter and younger than her poor father and all the hungry kind of men and women he now knew. In a bare year, Prague had changed. The city had become rueful and poor and her parents' friends appeared to be dwindling. She knew that sometimes her mother cried when she thought the children were asleep. She knew that the new thing in her father's face was fear.

But war was an adult problem. It was the grown-ups who were sad and diminished and frightened. They listened to radios and spoke furtively with each other on streets bare of soldiers. They prayed for the Americans to join their war. Impotently, they cursed and dreaded the Germans. But children seemed exempt from war. The adults were hungry and frightened but the children of Prague (Dana and Rachel) prevailed almost happily. Their games were more sombre and the word *German* had become an ugly, frightening word – a bogeyman the adults were too scared to mention. Dana grew up. One afternoon the three girls congregated in Dana's bedroom. She took off her dress and showed Rosza and Rachel her new puffed-up breasts and the hair that had grown between her legs. Rachel laughed and laughed until she fell off the bed and was sick on the floor. Dana was cross; her expected *coup de théâtre* had not gone well. Hotly, she told Rachel that she would have breasts soon and probably even more hair between her legs. Rachel laughed until her face was wet with tears.

Sometimes, the adults' anxiety disturbed the children's ease. There were stories of riots and fights. Of men and women being beaten and killed in the street. The soldiers broke windows and sometimes burnt shops and houses. Rosza did not know why they might do this but she believed the stories. One day a friend of her father had come to their house in tears. He had sat in their drawing room gnashing his teeth and wailing his wife's name over and over. Her mother had ordered the children out of the room but afterwards they could hear the man's choked voice loud in the house. His wife had been *taken*. Rosza remembered the woman well, a plump matron with crooked teeth and a lisp, whom Dana had mimicked to the delight of her sisters. That night when her father kissed her good night, his face was paler and older than usual.

Then they were moved to Theresienstadt. Her father stayed in Prague. The mother and the three children boarded a crowded bus and were driven to the old fortress town. At first, Rosza thought that their move to the ghetto was some shabby necessity, a consequence of her father losing his job. But after a few weeks Rosza's father still had not joined them. She knew then that something bad had happened. Her mother wept every night and her sisters were often sick and querulous. They lived in a verminous shack with two other families – an old couple from Vienna and an ill-conditioned Prague woman with her four children. It was dirty, crowded and smelt.

Rosza began to play a silent game with herself in which she pretended that her father was there with them. She heard the soundless words he spoke, his soft lost laughter. She pretended to ask him questions about where he'd been and chide him for being so slow in joining them. At night, she squeezed her grubby pillow to her chest and murmured to it like a daughter.

She knew her father was dead. Her game continued, none the less. Her father could and would come back like he did every day in her game. She would greet, question, chide and embrace him like she embraced her pillow. One day a man who had known her father arrived in the ghetto. He came to the house in which they lived. Dana and Rachel were both lying sick in the next room but Rosza was present when he told her mother that her husband was dead. The child rushed at him, screaming and hammering at him with her fists. The man gathered her up in his arms and tried gently to subdue her struggles. He left before she had tired of beating and scratching him.

They had been in Theresienstadt for much more than a year before Rosza realized why they were being harmed. She had known that she was Jewish since she was very small but it had been a loose knowledge, like knowing that the world was big or the sky was high. She had probably imagined the world a Jewish world for her world was so. But Theresienstadt proved that the world was not so.

They had been returning home with a loaf of bread for which Rachel had bartered one of her mother's rings. Rachel had hidden the bread in her ragged coat and she and Rosza walked quickly, their hunger and fear equal prompts to speed. They were going so fast that they had rounded the corner too far to stop even when they had seen the soldiers. The Germans were on both sides of the street, harassing everyone who passed by. Rosza quailed and moved to turn back but Rachel's hand prevented her. The two sisters walked on.

The soldiers were playful at first, so tall and healthy that they were amused by Rachel's puny stature. They mocked her in raucous voices, a group of them forming around the two girls. Even when they found the bread, their laughter did not abate. The young soldier who had found it, threw the loaf to one of his comrades. The second soldier held the bread as though giving it back to Rachel but when she stretched out her hand, he threw it to yet another soldier.

They played this game for a few minutes. Rachel was careful to respond each time they proffered the bread, she did not want to spoil their good humour. But they soon tired of their sport – it was a game they had often played. Someone threw the loaf to the young soldier who had found it in the first place. He muttered a foreign oath, dropped the bread to the ground and crushed it into the mire of the pavement with his heavy boot. Goaded and starving, Rachel bent to pick up what she could and the soldier swung his boot heavily into her face. She was thrown back, her head smacking the pavement with a clear thud. The other soldiers laughed louder and the group began to disperse, satisfied with this conclusion to their game. Rachel tried to lift herself but slumped back on the pavement. The young soldier cleared his throat idly and spat thickly on the injured girl. He motioned Rosza to take her sister away before he did. Rosza hurriedly helped Rachel to stand and, with her arms around her sister's waist, dragged her home.

Rachel died a few days later. She died weeping in pain. She was thirteen years old. Rosza had thought her father's death a game, an impossibility. Rachel's death was only death, death without revision or appeal. Her mother was struck dumb with grief. She could not weep, only her hands showed her pain as they worked, fingers tight in each other's empty grasp. Rosza's mother had suffered her limit now and her daughter's death had robbed her heart bare. She passed days and weeks in silent, hand-wringing grief, the pain chafing inside her. Her beauty remained like a shame to her.

Rosza could not bear her mother now. She began spending her days furtively wandering the ghetto. In Prague, the young and hale had walked the streets while the elderly had remained indoors, infirm. In Theresienstadt it was the young who stayed inside while the old patrolled the streets but everyone was ill, frightened and hungry. People were taken away on trains and more would arrive on trains. Once a load of drab, shaven-headed children arrived and were marched through the ghetto to an empty warehouse. They were deported the next day.

Dana was missing for days at a time. She was in love with a boy from Lidice. She was seventeen. The old spite that Rosza had admired had left her now. By the winter she was pregnant. By the spring she and her boy from Lidice had been taken away on one of the trains that now travelled east every day.

Rosza's last few months in Theresienstadt were nothing, grim sisterless absence. The residents of the ghetto were in stupor, none more than she. She was wretched without Rachel. Dana's womanhood had made the loss of her easier to bear but Rachel had died a child. Rosza's own puberty was late now, so late it seemed it wouldn't come. She was half starved and half grown. Her body seemed cataleptic and inert. It refused to grow.

Rosza and her mother were put on one of the eastbound trains. The carriage was a wooden cattle car. Within the first few hours, it was filthy and loathsome. There were one hundred and fifty Jews: men, women and children. The journey took three days. They stopped at a siding for a whole night because there was no engine available to pull the train. The youngest children died quickly. The old men and women died after a longer struggle. The reverse of what she might have expected. Rosza's mother did not speak in those three days. She lay mutely with her head in her daughter's lap while Rosza stroked her hair and murmured like Rachel had done for her.

They arrived early on a black, cold morning. The train lay still until dawn broke. Some of the other carriages had been emptied before theirs and Rosza could see files of naked Jews being marched away along the railway track. There were soldiers with machine guns, soldiers with sticks and batons, soldiers with fierce dogs and soldiers with clipboards. Men in outsize stripes like pyjamas helped the Jews off the train and made them huddle in a cold, frightened group near the open carriage door. The dead Jews were thrown from the carriage into a grotesque heap. Heavy Ukrainian Capos shoved the crowd of Jews, squealing orders at them. The men in the big pyjamas and the clowns' shoes were gentler, coaxing the Jews into calm. The Germans were impassive, bored and busy.

They were instructed to undress. Some women started crying. But the crowd was docile and obeyed. Rosza's hands shook as she struggled with her filthy dress. Close to her, some of those who had already undressed were old. So close and naked, their bodies were bizarre, distressing. Shrunken legs and distended bellies, pendulous breasts and flesh as dimpled as orange peel. She turned away. Her mother tried to smile at her.

She had never seen her mother naked before. She was astonished by her breasts, by the thick patch of hair between her thighs. She was beautiful, unreal and frightening. Rosza shivered. Hunger had not made her mother ugly like the other naked women. The girl pressed herself to her mother's breasts and felt her shoulders encircled by her bare warm arms.

An officer with a list was counting and noting the naked Jews. One of the Ukrainians approached him and mumbled something close to his ear. The German looked at the man with distaste but nodded assent to something. He seemed to labour under some lazy debt to the Ukrainian. The Capo approached the crowd of Jews. He inspected the women minutely, lingering over the younger ones. He approached Rosza's mother and stopped. He placed a rough calloused hand on her breasts and then slapped her buttocks appraisingly. He turned and called out to the officer with whom he had whispered. The officer looked up and nodded casually. The Ukrainian grabbed her mother's hand and pulled her away from the huddle of other Jews. Rosza stared in disbelief as he dragged her into the gap between two of the carriages. The man did not attempt privacy. Rosza watched as he started to maul and rub her mother's breasts and belly. He unbuttoned his trousers and pulled them down. The men and women who stood near Rosza tried not to look or listen. The counting officer continued counting monotonously. Rosza could only believe that someone would stop this thing. No one did.

ROSZA was among a small group of children who were smuggled out of the procession to the gas room. The camp's security had failed as the Allies had advanced closer in the past months. The Jews were growing more daring: the children were concealed in the infested barracks where the worker Jews slept. The men brought food when they could but they could spare little. Some of the children starved. Some died of typhus. Many merely died.

When the Allies entered the camps, the Germans had gone. They had marched away thousands of internees and shot thousands more. The corpses formed rotting hills. The Allied soldiers were incredulous and revolted. The surviving

Jews stared amazed at the healthy, well-fed soldiers. They fell upon the food they were given. The soldiers could not bear to watch them eat like dogs.

A soldier wearing a red handkerchief wound round his head, approached Rosza. He spoke to her in English and he was surprised when she answered him, haltingly, in that language. She could not tell whether he was American or British. His face was red and suffused with a strange expression. Gently, he raised his hand. She flinched and he murmured to calm her. He raised his hand again and tried to brush her matted hair away from her face.

'You're a girl,' he said.

She was alarmed to see that tears had filled his eyes and wondered what was wrong. He reached into the breast pocket of his shirt and pulled out a bar of chocolate. He offered it to her. She stared back at him, her face blank. He unwrapped a corner of the bar and bit a piece off, chewed and swallowed it. He offered her the chocolate once more. She shook her head. His tears were running now and he looked at her in bewilderment. Encouraged by his open, hurt face, she pointed at the red cloth tied around his head. Surprised, he took it off and held it out to her. She took it from him and held it close to her eyes. She felt that she had never seen such colour, such red. She rubbed it against her filthy cheek and smelt the man's sweet smell.

The soldier had broken down. He cried openly, his nose ran and his mouth trembled convulsively. Rosza was upset. His seemed a terrible grief. She reached out and gently patted his head.

'It's all right,' she said. 'It's all right.'

SHE stopped talking before dawn. Her voice had grown dry. Her ruined face was impassive – so broken that it was incapable of expression. He sat on the bedside chair, hugging himself with his lacerated fists. He watched silently as she limped into the bathroom. He listened to the small sounds of her washing and bathing her face and body. He knew that she was trying to hide as much as possible of her injuries before she had to face their son. The boy would wake soon. She had little chance of real concealment. Martin would know that he had beaten her.

When she returned, her face had improved little. She sat before her dressing-table mirror and brushed her hair away from her forehead with a shaking hand. She picked up a compact full of flesh-coloured powder and leaned forwards close to the mirror. She inspected her face minutely. She lifted the little cosmetic pad towards her face but paused half-way. No face powder could begin to hide her blemished flesh. She replaced the pad in the compact and turned towards her husband. Her voice was level and confident. She told him that she was leaving him.

OF course, it was Manfred who left in the end. He was dressed and ready in half an hour. He gathered some belongings and packed them in a small suitcase. Emma waited in the bedroom. When he was ready to leave, he went and stood by her chair. He stood there for a few moments, unwilling to touch her and uncertain what to say. Emma did not raise her head to look at him. He left then without saying goodbye.

He walked away from the house numbly. He had left the keys of the car with her as if in some pathetic atonement. He walked aimlessly south. He had crossed the river into Vauxhall by the time he became sensible of himself. There was a certain unlikely ache in him that was like bleeding or bereavement. He felt a kind of insensate optimism. It was not possible *surely* that he could suffer long like this. Something good, kind was bound to happen. It would all be better soon.

After a dazed day wandering around south London, he slept, exhausted, in a park near Putney. He woke continually, vaguely aware of some grand mishap. When day came and he was too cold to sleep further, grief arrived in full. He was winded and gasping at its open-eyed opprobrium. He felt mined and excavated with loss. A nascent shame formed in him.

He slept rough for four more tortured, wicked nights. Then he went to Tapper and told him what had happened (except for the beatings). Tapper gave him a great deal of money. He advised him to find somewhere to stay and then to telephone Emma. He seemed to think that the break was temporary.

EVENTUALLY, they met on a bench in Hyde Park from where they had once watched a cold disappointing dawn a few months before they were married. Manfred arrived at the bench before his wife and sat waiting for her. He saw her approach but when she hesitated he looked away. She sat beside him and waited calmly for him to speak.

He made a long, hard speech of reparation which, afterwards, he could never recall. Emma listened silently to his lists of regrets and promises. When he had finished, she did not speak. Surrendering to an ungovernable impulse, he turned his head and looked her full in the face. It was broken still. She rose immediately and walked away. He chased after and tried to hold her back, tugging weakly at the sleeve of her coat. Two bystanders, businessmen of some kind, saw the situation and grappled him to the ground. By the time he had convinced them that Emma was his wife, she had disappeared.

It took a week of pleading to gain another meeting. The venue was the same, the procedure identical, the blind condition just as implacable. The day was wintry and muted and his hands and face chapped and stiffened as he waited for her. This time he did not plead or promise. He had concluded that there was no expiation for him or her. He conjured a dream of future, repaired marriage in which he loved her as he had first loved her. This time he remembered all he said. He remembered it for many years even when time had rotted it into absurdity. Again Emma listened without speaking and when he finished he could hear only the rumble of distant buses and the shrill gabble of the birds in the trees. After a few silent moments, he turned and looked at her. Her face was less bruised and swollen now but it was crushed and small with pity, with pity for him. Manfred never saw her face again. He did not try to stop her when she walked away.

By the time they met again, Manfred had gone back to work and Emma had sold the car and started training to be a nurse. They agreed that they would not divorce. They arranged maintenance payments. Manfred begged to be allowed to remit an enormous portion of his income but Emma would not take it. After much pressing, she agreed that she and Martin would take half his salary until she qualified. The house was hers, naturally. Manfred tried to leave himself with nothing. His new flat was sparse and meagre, all that he owned apart from his clothes and some few of his books, he had left in Emma's house. He did not complain but hoped that Emma would notice anyway. She didn't notice and he was left with nothing.

Soon their meetings became habit. By unspoken agreement they were meeting once a month and he was telephoning once a week. The meetings were no curative for his new ills. Though he could not see her, he knew that the marks he had made on her face would fade. But his own hands, his wrecker's hands would never heal. Within six months his vigour had fled, damaged but precious. His decay was no story. It was the complete and only truth. He was stricken and haggard with his opposite of joy.

ELEVEN

MANFRED staggered biliously out of Mary's café. His lunch had been entirely indigestible. Mary had been particularly querulous. She had accosted the old man as he sat in a sudden grip of pain and had moaned at him for nearly forty heavy minutes. The old woman complained bitterly about the new infrequency of his visits. Now, standing wretchedly on the street outside her café, Manfred decided that he would not go back to Mary's. Time was too precious.

The streets were blue. Though the day was mild, the light was frozen indigo and violet. The city's objects were sharp in this light. The people's faces looked numb in its frost. The old man crossed the street, thick with slow cars.

Mary had told him how ill he looked. She had taken several satisfied minutes to describe minutely the extent of his decline. She advised him that he should see a doctor but informed him that she didn't think that this would do any good. Doctors were a waste of time. It was Manfred's own fault for not eating properly (meaning, in Mary's café).

The old man passed a television shop with a cardboard patch stuck to its broken window. A cricket match was being broadcast on a score of screens. The multiple movements, the flurries of green and white made him dizzy. He looked away and walked on.

In front of him, a young couple walked slowly, their arms draped negligently around each other's easy waists. They were having some good-humoured dispute. The young man disengaged himself from the girl's grasp. He turned away, arms wide in a gesture of theatrical exasperation. The girl flicked her hair and laughed behind her hand. They kissed ostentatiously, glad to share the drama of their youth and spirits. Manfred quickened his step and overtook them as speedily as he could.

He felt old. His limbs were cracked and weak. He felt heavy with postponed death. That morning he had written three wills and torn each of them to pieces. With so little to leave, it had seemed a foolish thing to do. The paucity of the legacy he would leave had depressed him. Suddenly, the prospect of Martin and Julia having a child did not anger him so much. He would at least have some sort of biological responsibility for that child. It would make some kind of mark. It left some trace of him.

Nearby, a group of children sat on some steps blowing soap bubbles at each other. A cat lurked between their feet, bewitched and frightened by the tiny pop of the bubbles bursting. The children laughed each time the cat jumped and flinched. One of the little girls, however, tried to stroke the animal, to reassure it. As he passed, Manfred winked at her. The child frowned and gripped the cat tighter. Manfred blushed.

The air was still and damp. At a height of three feet and above, nothing was happening. The distance between the sides of the street was sluggish with arrested air. People left their scents and warmths behind them, patches of perfume and pipesmoke as individual as ties or stockings. The old man's nostrils twitched with pleasure.

In the tobacconist's, he bought some cigarettes. The amiable Muslim owner chatted idly about the cricket match Manfred had seen in the television shop.

'Wish I was there,' the man said, his smile professionally wide. 'Stuck here. Have to make an honest penny. Hey . . .' his smile nearly split his face now '. . . maybe one day I retire and then I see all the cricket going.'

Manfred reflected a pallid version of the man's smile and handed him some money. A book lay face down on the counter. Craning his head furtively, Manfred read the title. It was a famously anti-Semitic tract about the great lies of Zion. It was a big Islamic favourite. A Jew-killing book. The old man wondered whether this friendly shopkeeper realized that his customer was a Jew. Would the cosy cricket chats have ceased? Manfred took his cigarettes and left the shop, not returning the man's farewell.

As always when he encountered any Jew-baiting, Manfred suddenly felt a little more Jewish. He had used to think such things remnants of old hatreds but he knew now that they were as pristine as any intolerance needed to be. Joyously apostate all his days, he was always Hebrew in the face of Gentile loathing. It was a reflex, like fighting for a smaller brother or like the tired gallantry of a reluctant beau.

A tall bus rolled noisily past. From a window on the top deck, two young girls waved and pulled foolish faces at the old man on the pavement beneath them. The world seemed boisterously Christian. Manfred thought of his Jewish wife. As usual, it was a sensual recollection. In the late hours of a hot night in their first summer, she stood remembered bending over the kitchen sink with a glass in her hand, wearing her green cotton dress with the buttons down the back. He found it interesting that men remembered women's clothing by their means of access, buttons, zips, hooks. She had always seemed more Jewish than he. The incautious Gentile comment or open taunt always wounded him on her behalf. He felt that it was she who was being slandered. The blood libel wounded her.

Close by, a record store blared disposable music. The banal vitality of the melody cheered him unaccountably. Unbidden, another memory of Emma's flesh arrived. A Sunday afternoon in the late summer of 1953, Emma lay naked on the bed, warm in the torpid light from the half-drawn curtains. She had told him that she was pregnant only the day before and already it seemed to Manfred that her belly was pushing taut as a drum. Her body seemed newly abundant and full. His penis hard as algebra, Manfred was hungry and gluttonous. He felt that they would never make enough love. Under his hands, her belly swelled, making him want her more.

Little shocks of bliss puckered the flesh on his arms and spine. It felt good to be old. To have such moments in storage. Outside the tube station a sturdy middle-aged tramp was slumped on the pavement, a greasy cap beside him. The man was singing 'Nobody loves me, I'm nobody's child' in an imperfectly disguised Roscommon accent. A meagre clutch of coins failed to glitter in his cap. A large black woman bustled past him, suddenly bending to drop something in the cap. The stocky beggar inclined his head elegantly without breaking from his song.

Now, after twenty years, he had begun to listen to what she had told him the night before he left. He spent a year learning what he could of the slaughter of the Jews. He read books filled with numbing lists of the repetitive dead. He watched murky old films showing groups of naked Jews being shepherded to their deaths. Some of Tapper's refugee tenants told him hard stories of what they had seen and heard.

He was astounded. Europe had grown an industry of death. They had rendered the fat from the corpses into tallow. The deathcamps had been candle factories – soap-shops. Lunatic with some reasonless rage or fear, they had tried to cull an entire race. The numbers were numbers, long and neutral. They had named it holocaust. Emma had lived it. It had been a different war from the war he had fought and lost. It had been Gehenna. It had been the place and time of burning.

He saw a set of pictures that had never been reproduced: they were considered too horrible. Another set of pictures had been completely prohibited. Apart from Emma, those like her and those who had liberated the camps, no one had ever seen them. He remembered an afternoon in a soldier's bar in Potsdamerstrasse in Berlin just after the war: a British newspaper had printed Nazi photographs of the camps. He remembered the youngest of the soldiers crowding round to ogle greedily at the groups of naked women. One boy groaned aloud and expressed a wish that he had been there among that flesh. It took Manfred thirty years to forgive that. They had probably never seen naked women before. It had been a response that belonged, however shoddily, to a healthier century.

After a few years he had stopped searching for words and pictures that described her holocaust. He even began to avoid it. It was an unknowable damage. But still, every night, he tried to dream it away for her. He tried to make it good, like a debt. The dreams of vengeance or rescue faded with age. He dreamed impossible dreams of benevolent Nazis, clement revisions in which the camps were as festive as holidays. It made a kind of sense at night, a blameless, bearable sense. But he knew that the comfort was his. He could not bear what she had borne. She was printed dark with old marks.

THE first few years of their separation were a postponement. He passed a couple of black years, dead autumn to dead autumn, numb with misery and shame. He found the flat in which he would live for the next twenty years and more. He grew accustomed to solitude. The routine of his loneliness soothed and aged him. Before he was fifty, he was stooped and old.

He missed her like pain. The first year was blind and grieving – an executed year, endured but scarce remembered. He sometimes wondered how he had managed to see out that numb space of loss. He had worked and lived, eaten and breathed but it was a black forgotten time.

They continued to meet as she had demanded. The veto she had placed on his looking at her remained. Originally, it had been because of the injuries to her face but as the months passed and those injuries healed, he was still not permitted to look at her. Once a month, he sat on the park bench, his face turned from her, his eyes blind and wet. He told no one of the nature of these meetings. Tapper knew that they met but he would not have dreamed that Manfred was not allowed to look at her. As a boy, Martin didn't even know that they met at all. Manfred knew that others would find their meetings absurd or foolish. Evidence of derangement, his or hers.

He had beaten her for living before and without him. He had beaten her for the harm *he* had not done. He had beaten her for the war. He had beaten her for her beauty, for her son, her silence and suffering. He had beaten her because he loved her. He had tried to crush something out of her. To make a shape he could love easier.

He searched for a way to understand. The smallness in him had gone. Without her, his life was more completely ruled by her than it had been before. She was his best parts. Each lonely moment in his dismal flat was a careful ritual of her absence. He felt tenderly monitored by his invisible wife. The fantasy that she saw and heard the solitary events of his life gave shape to his pointless time. But like a story, he knew that there would have to be an end, something conclusive and valedictory. A proof of love, of penance.

He knew now what she had seen reflected in the glass,

what she had seen in her face. She had seen harm done and harm suffered. She had seen Birkenau, the heaps of reasonless dead. She had seen her own face marked by his hands. She had seen a part of herself dead, as the unsurviving survivors seemed to. When he had beaten her, he had confirmed her victimship. He had buried her.

And though every day he tried to make it good, the thought of her suffering rotted in him. He tried to forgive himself. He tried to forgive *them*. One day he tried to count the Jewish dead. He sat in a chair by the window and counted as the day faded and the room darkened until it was black and silent except for the mumbled numbers of his toll. By the time he had counted twenty thousand, his mouth was dry and his throat felt swollen and gasping. At forty thousand, his mouth began to crack and bleed. It would have taken him a month of counting to count the first million and he would be struck dumb before that.

He searched for a way to understand. The ground was thick with the dead and the sky was dark with their ashes. The uncountable suffering dead. Like Emma, their weakness had been no weakness. Sometimes, he lay in bed at night and dreamed their legion murdered ranks. He believed that the dead could speak. He only hoped that they forgave.

'ARE you all right? Hello. Are you all right?'

He was sitting slumped on the steps of a shabby, broken house, a street or more from his home. A figure loomed above him as he held his grey head in his hands.

'Are you all right?'

Manfred looked up and saw Garth standing there, his expression solicitous. His face and figure were dark against the bogus glory of the sudden sunshine. He tried to smile weakly at the young man.

'I thought it was you,' Garth said. 'You look pretty grim. Are you feeling sick?'

'No. I'm fine. I felt tired for a moment.'

Garth looked unconvinced. 'Are you heading back to the flat?'

Manfred nodded. The young man sat down on the steps beside him. 'Well, listen. You get your breath back for a minute and then I'll walk back to the house with you. I was going that way, anyway. I'll be glad of the company.' His tone was bright and unassuming, skilfully implying no infirmity on Manfred's part. The old man was a little nettled by this professional manner.

'I'm fine now. We can walk.'

'Suits me.'

Garth stood up and waited for Manfred to rise without his assistance. The old man puffed and breathed hard but managed to stand straight without much difficulty. They moved off at a neutral pace, Garth stepping slightly ahead of his companion. They walked for a minute or so without talking. Manfred noticed that the street was full of children. They sprinted, skipped and sulked all over the place. Several times, Manfred and Garth had to step gingerly around some little group playing a complicated pavement game. The school summer holidays had just begun and these children were obviously glad to be on the street during the daytime. Manfred had been under the impression that children only watched television these days. He was glad to see that this was not true. Manfred turned to the young man walking beside him.

'Do you think I'm old?' he asked.

Garth smiled and looked at the pavement.

'You're not young,' he replied levelly.

'But do you consider me an old man?'

Garth stepped forward quickly and kicked a football back to a group of boys playing on some grass. He laughed, enjoying the sudden display of his own galvanic youth. He rejoined Manfred and then walked on for a few yards while he measured his response.

'You don't like being old?' he asked Manfred.

'When I was a boy I met a very old man who told me that he didn't understand why the world didn't get tired. I didn't know what he meant. But now I'm old, I'm tired and I'm wondering why the world doesn't get tired.'

Garth laughed.

'But it does. Don't you read the newspapers, man? The world's tired, all right.'

They turned onto the street where they lived. Across it, a man with two Newmarket greyhounds was opening his garden gate. His dogs were frothy with sweat and satisfaction. Manfred considered shouting a greeting but the man had entered his house before he had summoned courage and breath.

Garth spoke. 'I'm glad we're talking. You've been living underneath me for near two months and we haven't talked properly. I've seen you around a lot. Sometimes you make decisions about people before you really meet them. I'd figured that guy Webb for a geek. But you seemed all right. Always on your own, but you seemed OK.'

Manfred smiled a small smile. He was touched but he hoped that the young man was not going to follow this up with some advice about seeing a doctor. They were only fifty yards away from the house. If he could keep the conversation neutral until they were inside, he would be safe. He would plead weariness and say that he was going to bed for a while.

'You're sick, aren't you?'

They were walking under a small beech tree. The old man brushed some drooping branches away from his face. Garth ducked under the foliage and continued. 'I'm a nurse. I should know. That night on the stairs – you looked really bad. Liver? Pancreas?'

Manfred stepped off the pavement and began crossing the road to the house in which they both lived. Garth tripped after him.

'Yeah. I know. You don't like doctors. It's nothing serious. We've all got to go some time. But listen, if you've got some kind of deathwish let me give you some advice.' They had reached the pavement outside the house. Garth's hand on the old man's shoulder arrested his progress. They looked into each other's faces, young and old. 'Take a fistful of pills. Slit your wrists. Blow your brains out or jump in a river. Just don't let nature take its course. It's not nice. It's not nice at all. I've seen it. I really don't recommend it.'

He smiled an easy smile and raised his eyebrows coaxingly. Manfred opened the garden gate and walked up the path to the front door. The sunshine had fled and the afternoon was dull and flaccid once more. The old man opened the front door and held it ajar. He beckoned Garth, who shook his head tolerantly and followed him into the hall. Manfred closed the front door. Again both men stared at each other, uncertain, embarrassed. Garth waited for some reply. Manfred moved to the door of his apartment and brandished his key. He glanced back at Garth. It was kind of the young man even to notice. He could not be rude. He smiled.

'May I ask a question?' asked Manfred.

'Of course.'

Manfred turned the key in the lock and opened his door.

'Did you know I was Jewish?' he asked.

Garth smiled a wide, wide smile.

'Did you know I was black?'

Manfred laughed a big, big laugh.

By midnight, Manfred had begun to understand something of Garth's warning. Nature's course was violent and cruel.

The blight in him had grown vicious and revolting. For two hours he had wept in the bathroom as he crouched over the sink and the toilet bowl. His flesh had grown cold and loathsome. He vomited blood and bizarre colours of pulp and cess. He had puked green, a colour which terrified him. It seemed so unnatural, so unlikely. He presumed that it was bile and knew that he was in trouble.

Of course, the actual pain kept step with these new breakthroughs. Each new retch and expulsion was accompanied by dreadful cramps and twinges, each one more appalling than the last. He mumbled to himself in pain. He talked like a poet reading, monotonous and haggard. His heart and lungs felt clutched and squeezed by crisis. At two o'clock in the morning, he had decided that he would die before dawn. His old inelectric heart faltered and raced. His eyes were dark.

The madness ceased just before dawn. Abruptly, his body flooded with insensate calm. Only his breathing, the querulous rise and fall of his chest, proved that he was alive. He stumbled into the armchair by the window. The curtains were open. Stunned and numb, he stared out as the night ended and the street grew pale and cold with infant daylight. He smoked a tasteless cigarette, glad that he was still alive. He ran his hands over his body, marvelling at its resilience.

Soon, before the dark had dissipated, he was sleepy and cold. He crushed a cigarette into an ashtray. He knew that he was truly dying. Conclusively dying. He was frightened and no longer glad. He would be dead in days. That was monstrous and sickening. But he was tired now. Sleep was more important. He could happily die tomorrow if only he could have some good, good sleep. He tried to rise from the chair and go to his bedroom but his legs and arms were weak and useless. He fell back and fumbled for another cigarette. Before he found it he was asleep and dreaming.

TWELVE
(1962–)

FOR more than twenty years they lived apart. The protocols of their meetings became refined and inviolate. Repetition was magical to them both. Twelve times a year they met in the park. After the first two or three years, Manfred forgot that he had ever tried or wanted to look at her during these meetings. Her invisibility took on a virtuous unreason, perfect and imperfect. Manfred was glad to submit himself to Emma's rules. He was content to follow any doctrine of fidelity.

For more than twenty years he was allowed to telephone her weekly. He soon flouted this restriction. He would call her when his loss and loneliness threatened to crush him. Apart from those agreed calls, Emma would not speak to him but she would never hang up immediately and Manfred was able to gabble through the words he had to speak. He knew she didn't listen but it was a relief of sorts. Soon, he called her so often, so fruitlessly, that he was no longer able to pay his telephone bills. His telephone was removed. He then relied on public telephones. Daunted by publicly pleading with her, the unlicensed calls decreased and then ceased entirely.

Twenty years and more; a league of nights as Manfred withered alone in his venerable bed. He grew old. His face was rubbed worn and his body chipped like an ancient statue. His belly, once fine and strong, soon folded and wrinkled under the weight of the hostile years. Every day, his vigour ebbed a little more. His musculature slackened, his bones tightened. His penis, never prodigious, receded like a button mushroom. But Manfred was unashamed of his ageing. His body's decline seemed fittingly penitent. He was even glad that, each month, Emma saw him decay so, that she should notice this grim reparation.

Martin grew older. Unlike many fathers, Manfred was unsurprised by his son's manhood – he had been a very imperfect boy. Adulthood sat better upon him. His gravity seemed less grotesque in the man. He visited Manfred every few weeks and the old man watched him grow without interest. Their talk was always desultory and neither ever spoke of Emma or what the boy might have seen or heard. Martin went to university. He met Julia. Martin left university. He married Julia. Son and father aged further apart. A neutral, felicitous distance developed between them. The gap was loveless and austere and any buried feeling between them rotted in the ground. The son's unspoken grudges wore away to a memory of resentment and the father's disappointment faded.

Some of the more-than-twenty years tasted sour to the memory. Some of them tasted sour as need be at the time. He was an old Jew. He was an insult. Wifeless, bereft, he felt stopped up, broken and rejected. Time passed him like vinegar and salt. It was useless time, endured, suffered. He blamed the war. He blamed the century. He nearly blamed the weather.

In that more-than-twenty years, the last of the old man's friends died. Spike was found dead in his grubby bathroom, Tapper's fatty heart capitulated on his fifty-fifth birthday and Manfred's surviving brother died in the cancer ward of a Boston hospital. Manfred was astounded by the extent of his grief at the loss of Tapper. He realized how much rough love he had stocked up for his dead employer. Tapper had been predominantly shady if not actively criminal. He had often lived off amoral earnings, he had conned and mastered everyone he had ever met (including Manfred).

He had lived without sorrow or happiness. He had dealt and profited, the model of the moneyed halfman. His prideless self-promotion was his only exertion. Manfred and Spike had been his only friends and they had worked for him. Tapper had no use for friends. He worked hard not to make any, even inadvertently. But Manfred found his memory to be stocked with snub-nosed studies of Tapper's thin head from all angles. Perhaps it was the man's very lovelessness that made Manfred tender. He wasn't sure but on the day that he stood over the long hole into which Tapper's body was lowered, he grieved with uninvited grief.

The business had died with Tapper. Manfred worked on for another few months, trying to retrieve something from the necrotic mass of Tapper's affairs. Nothing much was left. Tapper had died just in time. The firm was rotten with debt and fraud. Manfred was amazed by how much Tapper had done without his knowledge. He was astonished to find that Tapper had been making an annual charitable bequest. A considerable sum had been sent to a European Zionist organization every year. Tapper's fake Jewishness had obviously gripped him to the end. Such a secret gesture was bizarre. It could have done nothing to support his public game of Judaism. The old game had become private, more real than not.

Manfred paid off the surviving remainder of the meagre workforce. Alice, the now middle-aged secretary who had pined so long in her secret fantasy of one day being Mrs Tapper(stein), was vehement in her denunciation. According to her, Tapper had always been an obvious brigand. No gentleman would have dressed or spoken like him. In the thwarted passion of her slander, she even hinted that her former employer had been improper in his behaviour towards her. Manfred could not decide whether her anger was a betrayal or a consolation for her loss. Whichever, Alice was firm in demanding twice as much severance pay as any of Tapper's other employees.

With the help of several squads of colourless money-men, Manfred wound up Tapper's company. At that time, the country was full of dying businesses. Manfred was glad that it was over. It had been a parasite's living. Nothing had been made except money. Tapper's dream, like all his dreams, had been an arid one.

Manfred retired, only a couple of years before he had intended. He had ensured that his pension had survived the accountants' corpse-stripping. Without the distraction of employment, he felt that he would dwindle and decay further. A penance such as his needed all his time, all his hours. Soon, he felt as redundant as he had hoped. There was no occupation to mitigate the asperity of his days. The only structure left to him was the schedule of monthly park-meets and the weekly telephone calls with his invisible wife.

Emma prospered. In the more-than-twenty years, her career grew more and more distinguished. She left the Middlesex Hospital, where she had trained, and went to work at St Thomas's. She campaigned for women's clinics, for screening, for a greater complement of women doctors. She published a report on private nursing. She sat on committees. Her name began to appear regularly in the newspapers that Manfred didn't read. She became famous in a tiny dignified way; always infuriating journalists by her refusal to allow her picture to be taken. Once, she even appeared on a radio programme. Manfred recorded the programme and replayed it endlessly for months. He was wounded by how different her voice sounded. The wariness that he was accustomed to hearing in her words had gone and her voice, boosted and deepened by the studio, was intimate and alluring. Jealousy and loss galled him like an ulcer. Eventually, he threw the tape away.

But her success, her stature, caused him less pain now.

Indeed, it scarce hurt him at all any more. He loved her with a better love. She was free of him and thus he could love her without greed. Without his eyes, he struggled to find a new blind way of loving her. Now that he could not see her, he realized how much he had loved her through his eyes, for the way she had looked. Apart from annual estimations of what the passing year might have done to or for her face, of what new beauty he might have missed, he loved without pictures.

Her absence strengthened his love. So much without her, he could love with no good reason and that was the only kind of love worth loving. She was entire without him, complete and other. He loved her by proxy. Wounded heart to wounded heart. He had once thought, after the harm had started, that he had loved her too much, losing himself in her. Later, alone, he knew that he had lost her among the cushions of his self-love. He had loved her for himself.

He settled into the living, vivid beauty of mediocrity, the life of a man without Emma. He became like other men, other old men. He welcomed the afflictive years. He felt himself grow into the shape of the old men who had always moved him when he had been a boy. Old men with tender shaved necks and sparse cropped hair, trundling the streets in dark soft clothes. Men he imagined to have no lives, no pasts – just old. He himself was probably provoking the same tenderness now. It suited him. He spurned no pity now.

Once, a couple of years before Tapper's death, in an incautious moment, Manfred had hoped. He had been looking over a large house that Tapper had purchased in Liverpool Road. When he had finished his work he had stopped for some coffee at an Islington tea-shop that Emma had liked. It was only streets away from their house. The proximity to his old house had unsettled him badly but it was the tea-shop that did it. The pale wooden chairs and tables, the deep green of the tablecloths, the rattle of the crockery, the hush of the chatting tea-drinkers, the wide light that filled the room, that bright, ultimately *possible* light. In a world so moderate and exquisite, everything was possible, even likely. He had inflated with confidence and joy. Life had too many aches of its own without adding extra needless anguish. Living without Emma was such an injustice, a crime against nature. With his big love, all he had to do was finish his coffee, walk the five-minute walk to the house he had bought for her and make her his. They were both older and damaged now. Much would be forgiven. He could be whole again. The wound of his loss would heal.

By the time he had paid for his coffee, the euphoria had faded. Some faults were beyond repair. Emma was unopposable. The face she would not show him was foul with suffering, with the untellable. There was a remnant in her from that age of atrocity in which she had lived. It was more than Manfred's cruelty that she had to forgive.

THE more-than-twenty years were more than twenty years. They were an aggregate of small beauties and better love. They were mornings, meals and cigarettes. They were unheard words. They were skies and streets and people. They were unwritten letters and hard hours, long and short. Without Emma, his life filled with her. He burned without return. The world grew tired and he passed the thin time of twenty years like a witness, refining the unrecorded testimony of his great, great love.

THIRTEEN

ARLY, before the day was full and the sun was high, Manfred realized that he would die that day. Summer had come and the air was warm and odorous. The sky was clear, high and blue as music. From his window, the street looked like a beach. The pavements were bleached with heat and dust and the youngest of his neighbours walked slowly and happily, their shirts and skirts as bright as paper. Cars glittered like shields in the shadeless glare of the street and his room filled with rumourous noise and light.

A new pain had come. It was a smaller, slighter pain but it was a final pain none the less. Inside him, deep in his belly, some vital thing had died. He knew that he bled somewhere in the blind halls of his flesh. He had vomited less that morning, but he had retched only blood. There had been no matter, no rejected food or secret bile among that red. It had been blood, simple blood.

It surprised him. He felt betrayed, incurable. He had even wept. He did not feel ready. He had not prepared. He mustered a sense of loss. Dying seemed much less elegant and inevitable now. He would see no more mornings. The thought appalled him. Before the night was out, he would simply cease. During the war he had watched the dead men. In Libya, in Egypt and Italy, he had watched them not move, not speak and not breathe. It had seemed a simple thing. If he had died then, his death would have been easy with so many companion dead. He could have not moved, not breathed and not spoken almost happily. But now he was old. He was solitary and grieving. His death seemed a bigger thing now. An event of import. Something to fear.

Then he wept. He wept for hours. He sat on the chair by his window and watched the bright street as he cried. Every few minutes some beautiful thing would occur, some minor comely event. An indolent dog with a smug expression would shift its prone body to bask more effectively on some baked pavement. Melodic laughter would erupt and subside from the window of a neighbouring house. Women carried bags of shopping, their shoulders hunched in the heat. Radios chuckled snatches of music. Children shouted. Women walked. Men talked. Old men wept.

He wept for himself. He wept for Emma. Love surged in him, flooding his damaged heart. No world could be big enough or good enough to house her. He felt that he was concluding his love for her. He was extending love to its furthest deepest region. He could love her no more than he loved her now.

She had been most beautiful when marred, strongest when weak. She had been various and complete beyond paradox. She had loved him when he had tried to crush the love out of her. She had left him wounded but she had given him Pisgah, she had given him all his dreams.

Once, just before they were married, he had waited to meet her at Notting Hill tube station. They were going to a cinema. He had been early and had sat on a bench and waited for her, warmed by low swathes of evening sunshine. He watched as each train stopped and disgorged its passengers, craning his head to find her. The longer he waited, the happier he grew. The crowds of people were marvellous, bright and multiple. Curiously, he was not disappointed by each of them that was not her. He had never felt so young. Some bizarre, reasonless joy filled him as he watched them. When Emma arrived, she was baffled by his mood. Normally reserved in public, he embraced her extravagantly, he kissed her. People stared at them, some smiling to see their ardour. That night he was too happy to go to a cinema. They just walked. They walked the warm streets as night fell and London grew bright with little lights.

To quell the thoughts of his wife, the old man tidied his flat in a desultory manner. It was pointless work. The flat was tidy already – it was needlessly, pitiably tidy. But the absurdity of such work cheered him. Again, death seemed like the jocund prospect that it had been for so many months. The neatness of his flat made him feel small and mortal. The meagreness of his belongings also moved him. His paltry furniture, his useless documents and miscellaneous papers were banal, the textual sum of a half-lived life. His garments were too few and too dull to be poignant. His books lay unread and his few photographs were neutral, memories without comment – his dead parents, his dead brothers, his living son and a few accidental friends, those, too, mostly dead. His one photograph of Emma moved him no longer. As he tidied it away, he waited for some flush of regret or dread. There was a certain frugal sadness but for a man who had loved like him, it was a squib, a come-down.

But soon his mood grew almost celebratory. The new crisis in his gut became almost manageable. It was his last day. A special event by any reckoning. He felt like having a leaving party or sending himself a deathday card. He searched for some gesture to mark this, the last of all his days. He thought of eating but he was weary of his diet of fibrous refuse and ponderous bread. He would have poured himself a drink if he thought he could have kept it down.

AROUND four o'clock the old man suffered another collapse. Briefly, he had thought it was the final crisis. He had sunk to his knees and his head had fallen forwards to the floor. Lying there, he had vomited strange colours, the last alloys from his dying gut. Later, when he was cleaning the rug, an idea for a valedictory gesture struck him. He would masturbate. Later still, lying sideways on his bed, penis in hand (both now wrinkled to an almost equal degree), he had a better idea. It was, in some ways, the only idea. He would call Emma. Even though it was not the appointed day, he would call her. He had something he wanted to tell her.

At five o'clock, he watched from his window as Webb returned from his day's nameless business. Manfred ducked behind the curtain so his neighbour might not see him. He heard Webb shouting coruscating abuse at some youths who had sat on his car. He heard the front door bang and looked out again. The sunshine was still strong on the street. Unlike the old man, it showed no sign of dying.

He made himself a pot of coffee. He prepared it carefully. It had to be decent. The thing that irritated him about death was that nothing seemed finished except him. The old man had always hoped that, at the close of his life, his life would feel concluded. That all the strands of that life, thick and thin, would have been gathered up and tied secure. But now, though he felt himself truly concluded, the rest of his life was half finished or less. As he drank his (mediocre) coffee, he was plagued by thoughts of incompletion.

By six o'clock Manfred's flesh was chill and damp. A mist of cool sweat lay on his forehead and scalp among the roots of his hair. This was strange since his interior body felt livid and molten with heat. A deadly conflagration worked under his ribs and as the day passed, the fire was rising slowly, scorching his heart and lungs. It hurt to a degree that astonished him.

When Garth came home from work, he had knocked

on Manfred's door. When the old man answered, Garth's face had betrayed his surprise.

'Old man, you're looking bad,' he had said.

'Don't I always?' Manfred had replied.

Garth had not lingered and their exchange had been perfunctory but, without reason, it had made Manfred feel less lonely. He was fond of Garth, who had been consistently kind. The old man felt that he should have been able to say something final to his neighbour but he could think of nothing suitable.

AT seven o'clock a door slammed and he woke suddenly. He watched Webb saunter away down the street and cursed himself for sleeping. He wasn't even tired. It was merely indolence. He rubbed his face with his hands. His skin was dry now. It felt papery and light under his fingers as though his flesh itself was fading away. The old man smoked a cigarette. He had to stay awake. He had things to do. His brief slumber caused him despair. He could not afford to sleep. He could not afford to die so.

EIGHT o'clock. Outside, people were on the street again. Couples walked slowly, their arms interclasped in varying attitudes. Groups of men marched in wide formations in search of public houses. Cars hummed and groaned by. People were going out. Even the daylight was more leisurely. It had lost its brassiest components. Now the sky was muted and gentle over London, its colours a cheap confection. Night was a couple of hours away. The old man waited keenly for the interval between day and day, that thing that had so frightened his father.

*

By nine o'clock the sky was true twilight. It had grown gaudy with colour and certain fleshy scrolls of cloud. The street was quieter now. Here and there, men and women stood on their steps and watched the complex sky. In his bathroom, Manfred urinated, washed his face, vomited, brushed his hair, vomited again, almost fainted and stared at the reflection in his mirror for more than thirty slow, slow minutes.

At ten o'clock, checking that his key was in his pocket, Manfred closed the front door of the house. It was dark now. The sky was purple and bruised blue. The air was thick with evening smells. After the day's heat, the trees exhaled vegetable breaths and their leaves swished softly in the breezeless air. The streetlamps were lit. Fringed by the leaves of their neighbour trees, they shed shaggy shadows on the pavements. Insects buzzed around them, momentarily gold or silver in their glare.

It took him nearly thirty minutes to reach the telephone box. His pace was slow and laborious. His legs shook as he walked and he already felt predominantly dead. Standing in the phone box, his nose wrinkling at the violent, human smell, it was many minutes before he was able to pick up the telephone and dial Emma's number. He was frightened. The plan to telephone Emma had been a good one. It had given him a goal for the day. But he knew that when he had spoken to her, he would have to face that other irrevocable goal.

Manfred picked up the telephone. He dialled the number and held the receiver to his ear. He heard the ringing tone, his heart flushing at the sound. The dialling tone choked abruptly as Emma's telephone was picked up. Manfred swallowed hard and began to speak.

Near twenty years before, his son, then a boy, had told him what happened when he telephoned his wife. The boy had been angered by some incautious gaffe on his father's part. Hard with the pride of still living with Emma, Martin told his father what Emma did when Manfred called her. Apparently, when she realized who the caller was, she lowered the telephone away from her ear until her elbow rested on her belly, the telephone pressed mute between her breasts. She would remain so while Manfred spoke — the only sound, a faint, inconsequential scratching noise from her bosom. When the muffled scratching seemed to have slowed or ceased, she replaced the telephone gently on its cradle. Later when the boy touched the dead telephone, it was still warm from her body.

THE sky was moonless and dirty, more brown than black as the old man walked back home. He could see the light in the doorway of his house, a hundred yards distant. Hours seemed to have passed since he had spoken to his wife. The return walk had been nightmarish, absurd. He had lost the last sovereignty over his body. His steps had been automatic. A big dark grasp twisted and gripped his gut. Perhaps it was Death itself, that fiend, that thief. The thought no longer cheered him and he sweated dread and fright.

His pain had been transfigured. It had become a theory of pain; a black ideal. It murdered him with its fullness; its complete, dreadful rectitude. Fearful of dying on the street, the old man summoned a parody of strength and stumbled the last few yards towards his home. A dog shouted mournfully and across the street a controversy between cats was briefly audible, yowl and grumble. The old man reached the path to his door. He stumbled forward, his arms flying out to break his fall.

★

WHEN he regained consciousness, he found himself lying on the doorstep. His legs sprawled inertly beneath him and his head rested near the foot of the door. For some moments he was groggy, unsure quite how alive or dead he was. A sudden afflictive wrench in his belly chafed him into certainty. He was enraged by his fall, by this indignity. But he was glad that he was not yet dead. Despite having called Emma, this night's remnant of life still felt unfinished.

He looked about him. The night was leaden. The trees and hedges were noiseless now, occasionally feathery in the brilliance of the streetlighting. He doubted whether he could move again. He was glad, at least, to die outdoors. A street, however quiescent or dismal, had more resonance and more drama than any of his four walls.

This close, he feared death. Sure terrors attended there. The half-remembered mumblings of a hundred rabbis: stories of loss, remorse and anguish. Impartial, unChristian Manfred slowed his already slow breaths. Another dog hooted its hollow call. The old man slumped further as a car passed, its headlights waving a dingy band of light across the street. To his hazy surprise, Manfred found that he didn't want to die at all. A crisis of pain scratched at his ribs and he began to weep.

Emma would live. That was barely fair. He thought of the telephone call, of his last few words muffled between her breasts. He thought of her warmth lingering on her telephone. Tonight he had imagined that warmth steal through to the receiver he held in his own hand. Emma would live. She would continue to leave her living trace on these actual objects. It was almost an infidelity. For the first time in more than twenty years, Manfred resented his wife. It seemed hard to die. It seemed very hard indeed.

Moths, gnats and other tiny night-fliers swerved and dived in the diffuse glow from the hall light of the house that Manfred lived in. The old man lay in the centre of their jerky orbit, his face and hands brushed by their tiny wings. His sudden anger had liberated him. He had grown weary of his serfdom to the lyric notion of his victimwife. His idea of her had become a brittle ideal. Now his anger had hardened the marshy texture of his love. It was stronger stuff. It paid her the compliment of allowing her to be real.

His tears had ceased. He raised his hand to his face and another cluster of moths glittered into the air. The insects were marvellous in their bright turbulence. Flashing against the black sky, they seemed the stuff of life itself. The old man was moved by their tiny beauty. He turned his face against the wall, pressing his hot skin against its cool. So close, the wall loomed massive and redoubtable. It seemed absurd in its solidness, its infinite, substantial brick. Such matter would survive him. He squinted at the bricks sympathetically. The thought of his death elated him once more. The thought of life prevailing so massively without him overjoyed the old man. Animate and inanimate, the moths and bricks would see him out. Emma, too, would be tenant of this Manfredless world. He lay, brute with joy, with the great benevolent indifference of godless life.

The night air was thickening with incipient moisture. The street was beginning to look soupy. The streaks of light from the streetlamps were more individual, defined and limited by the clogging air. The night was sluggish, moderate. Manfred was disappointed. He could have hoped for more vehemence from his last night.

Beneath him, his legs had recovered from their fall. They felt sensate again. But it made no difference. Manfred was tired now. His will had drained. His weariness had an inflexible allure. He would not get back into his flat. He would never see it again. At least it was tidy.

Across the street, he could see a figure lurching drunkenly from one pool of streetlight to another. Although the man's path was oblique, he seemed to be heading towards

Manfred. When the man stopped by a lamp-post to spit thickly, Manfred realized that it was Webb. The man launched himself across the road, stumbling badly. Manfred saw the gleam of a bottle in his hand. His heart sank.

Webb came to an abrupt stop. He had spotted Manfred and, for a moment, he seemed taken aback to find someone there. He tried to stare intently at the prone figure, the attempt doomed by the sottish swaying of his body. When he was sure of Manfred's identity, he laughed delightedly.

'Manny? Manny! What's gone on? Bad night for it. Been out? Say no more. Find me key. Have drink. Here.'

He stumbled towards the step where Manfred lay and collapsed in a sodden pile beside the old man. He cackled madly at his own discomfiture and dragged himself into a sitting position, his hands gripping Manfred's body for drunken purchase.

'Lovely down here. No problem. Little drink. Ha ha!'

He was obviously pleased to see Manfred in such informal circumstances and evidently laboured under the fraternal impression that Manfred, too, was intoxicated and had fallen there in his attempt to open the front door.

'Out on the piss? Quiet man. Know all about it. Night's young. Feel better in the morning. Get your gob round this. Dog that bit you.'

Webb proffered his bottle, thrusting it into Manfred's face and dropping it into the old man's grasp. Whisky spilled over Manfred's coat and shirt. Weakly, he tried to push the bottle away and wipe the alcohol from his clothes. Already, his numbed belly was wet. He wished he could protest but he could barely speak now. His lungs felt empty and useless, his tongue, a thick, lolling thing.

'Whoops! Dry fine. Good booze. Sure you won't? Don't mind help self. Nothing like.' Webb's features were dead with drink. His eyes were bloody and ulcerous. His mouth dribbled uncontrollably and his chin was wet and glistening in the light from the doorway. 'Gone rain. You stay? Catch flu not careful. Drink warm you.'

To Manfred's horror, Webb seemed to be settling himself down for a long exchange. He shifted his coarse body into a more comfortable position and rested his head against the wall beside Manfred. All Manfred's plans for an elegant, private death were destroyed. He had not imagined dying to Webb's gross accompaniment. The injustice was monstrous. He had done nothing to merit this. Impotently, Manfred raged. Lying satisfied beside him, Webb oozed woozy comradeship.

'Good see you, Manny. Do it more often. Think about you. All time. Am a bollocks. Wise man knows own father. Mean well. Stick together. Friends are for.'

Thorns twisted in Manfred's gut, shredding flesh and organ. A limitless, galled wound opened in him. He winced. His spine tingled and his skin pricked in the sheer terminal euphoria of this pain, this opposite, this death. His mouth tasted blood and his tongue felt open and molten. Even Webb noticed that the old man had jerked rigid and ecstatic.

'Manny! Manny? All right? Look bit black. Drop too much. All been there. No sweat, Manny boy. Have drink. Manny?'

Webb bent his head towards Manfred's to hear the words that the old man was trying to spit at him.

'What? Can't hear. Manny? Don't want me call you what? What? . . . Oh. Aren't we grand? *Manfraid*. Certainly, sir. Manfraid. Don't mind if I do.'

The old man slumped back, exhausted by his exertion. Weakly, he writhed with hatred. He mumbled some wordless curse at Webb and his eyes closed. Death felt heavy upon him. His limbs were leaden with its weight and underneath him, the ground felt like a thin skin through which he would fall. The sensation was horrible. He felt that he was moments away from his death and dry tears of fury scorched his eyes.

Webb talked on in the drunk's happy monologue.

'The nigger in? What's name upstairs. Ask a stupid question. He friend of yours? Black bastard. Never should let them in, I say. Fucking wogs. Shit for brains. Take jobs white men. Women, too. Take I mean. Buggers.'

He fumbled with the damp crotch of his trousers and leant on one side, facing away from Manfred. Producing his penis, he urinated from where he lay. Manfred heard the hiss of piss landing in the little garden beyond the steps.

'Don't mind, Manny. Sorry. Mandread. Seen all before. 'Tween friends. 'Nother drink. Out as quick as in.'

His piss finished, Webb shook his little member affectionately and stuffed it, still wet, into his trousers. As he turned onto his back, the old man beside him began to choke and retch dry. Webb punched him on the shoulder as he thrashed and jerked in desperate spasms. Webb's face assumed an imprecise expression of fellow feeling.

'That's it. Get it up there. Go on. Old hand. Know what it's like. Have drink. Feel better. Line stomach for you. No problem.'

The retching subsided. Viscous sweat lined the old man's face. A faint breeze on his cheeks revived him. Webb's face loomed nauseatingly close. The man seemed enormous suddenly, city-sized. Manfred could count the pits and pores of his thick face. His expression was a grotesque pantomime of concern.

'Better now? Told you. Drop too much. Puking never killed man. Right as rain morning. Didn't laugh you'd cry.'

Webb's face veered away, satisfied. Manfred's death was safe with such a poor scrutineer. There would be no last-minute rescue on Webb's part. Already, there was another eruption in his belly. His organs were flooding and drowning in some thick cold black. The old man steeled himself against his panic. Webb laughed his short, mad laugh and tried to sit up.

'Can't stay here. Things do people see. Where's the party, Manny boy? C'mon. Go a club. Few drinks. Some girls. Whatnot in the bathroom. Old as you feel.'

He punched his friend amiably and fell backwards unconscious, his head hitting the door with a dull thud. For a few extraordinary moments, the street was quiet. The rumble of distant London faded and there was magical, delicate silence. Soon, however, Webb started to snore. Manfred looked at him. The noise was remarkable. His mouth was open and wet, his lips oscillating when he exhaled. Again, the man looked like a beaten, remorseful old dog. His breathing rasped and chuffed. He sounded more dead than Manfred.

Gingerly, Manfred removed the heavy hand that Webb had left trailed across the old man's ribs. Manfred decided that he would miss Webb as much as he would miss anything. Webb, in his grossness, in his unalloyed appetite, seemed like the vivid principle itself. He was a sweaty, urinous exemplar of animate existence. Unconscious, drunk and snoring, Webb was the livable. The man was entire. There was something faintly grand in his unconscious, prevailing presence.

Another rage of pain. London's noise burst back. Grim shrieks filled his skull. A new pattern of cramps wrung his stomach and chest. His eyes clouded red and black and the world rained blood. Chafed and foul, his innards blew like bombs. His heart suddenly felt how a heart is – just a dumb, frantic muscle. That organ capered madly and his womb of pain was berserk in him.

The old man felt big fear. A black hand closed his eyes. His legs kicked convulsively and he sobbed for desperate breath. He tried to shout but his throat was blocked and useless. He panicked, floundering in the shallow water of faithless death. The skin-thin ground seemed to bulge and sag beneath him, close to snapping. His scrabbling hands clutched in spastic frenzy. Though his mind boiled in ferment, the world seemed simpler now. There was just this. This dying. This death.

Suddenly, the pain ebbed like water. His rheumy tears stopped and he felt like laughing. A car door *woofed* shut, a horn sounded and there was laughing and footsteps. The street seemed symphonic. He thought of Emma again. He could summon no grandeur. He thought of his body being discovered lying there beside the drunken Webb. It was a ludicrous position. Not without a certain grotesque panache. The old man cackled weakly until he wheezed. After all the forthright tragedy, he was glad that there were some jokes at last.

His breathing was a series of struggling gasps now but Manfred's pain was over. His body felt broken but anodyne. He would not now die of pain. As he haggled for breath, he knew that it was *this* bargain that would end. His air would stop shut and his life would starve away for oxygen. A period of unconsciousness followed by cessation of organs, systems and soul. A modest task, he thought.

And now it began. Deep in the very middle of him, some crucial valve warped, buckled and blew. Sweat stung his eyes blind and he felt warmth on his legs as his bladder emptied itself. His eyes cleared as he fought to breathe. The streetlights shone like distant flares. In his hand he noticed that he had grasped and torn away some of Webb's sparse hair. In the soft light from the porch, he noticed the bulk and grain of a nearby tree. The moths patrolled around him. Across the road, a garden gate was open, its paint chapped with age. He had hoped for valediction in these sights but it seemed death was much too busy a thing for that. The road seemed soft and black in the dim light. The moths sped and dived like time.

For a few seconds, the old man breathed on. Then something in his chest snapped shut and he drowned for air.

His teeth clacked as he gulped instinctively. His mouth filled with blood he could not taste. He snorted hard through his nose and inhaled a thin stream of air. His panic was pure now, concussive, almost dispassionate. His scrambling thoughts calmed as death pressed him. He snorted frantically and the ground-skin stretched paperthin under him.

Desperately now, he searched his mind for the thing that he promised he would think at the end. But he could only comprehend the street, the nigrescent dark and the squadrons of moths falling bright like snow. He sniffed vehemently. His hands touched the man lying beside him. Webb. He remembered. Then he remembered Emma. His wife. The whole point. He was dying for her. He tried to think harder. He had just told her he was dying, talking fruitlessly to her dumb breasts. She had been his wife, his painful wife. He fought the hallucinatory spasms. There was a reason in her. A reason for this. His death was a consequence. Nothing happened without cause.

His last breath had gone and when he snorted again, his head and throat were closed fast. His head filled like a balloon. A great cancerous bulge appeared on his neck. He touched it with the last of his strength. A long pity filled him as his last moments of airless thought sped away. The ground was breaking beneath him. He would fall now. He would die. With lastpage grace and fixity, his eyes closed. Unafraid now, he was delivered. Near the exit he saw her true soul, the soul that God would love for eternity.

AUTHOR'S NOTE

Emma still lives. When I am in the city I see where I can, when I can. My heart fills at the sight of her, with an ache and a joy that is slow to leave me. Emma is old now. She is free of much of her ancient grief. Though old, she has changed little and her beauty still startles, still arrests. Without her, my city, my world would be less. With her there is joy but there is much sadness. With her there is Profit and Loss. There is Wait and See. There is my pain. There is Manfred's Pain.